FURY

FURY

a novel

CLYO MENDOZA

Translated by
Christina MacSweeney

SEVEN STORIES PRESS
NEW YORK · OAKLAND

First published by Editorial Almadío in Mexico in 2021.

English translation © Christina MacSweeney, 2024

Seven Stories Press
140 Watts Street
New York, NY 10013
www.sevenstories.com

Library of Congress Cataloging-in-Publication Data

Names: Mendoza, Clyo, 1993- author. | MacSweeney, Christina, translator.
Title: Fury / Clyo Mendoza ; translated by Christina MacSweeney.
Other titles: Furia. English
Description: New York : Seven Stories Press, [2023]
Identifiers: LCCN 2023018580 | ISBN 9781644213711 (trade paperback) | ISBN 9781644213728 (ebook)
Subjects: LCGFT: Novels.
Classification: LCC PQ7298.423.E522 F8713 2023 | DDC 863/.7--dc23/eng/20230428
LC record available at https://lccn.loc.gov/2023018580

College professors and high school and middle school teachers may order free examination copies of Seven Stories Press titles. Visit https://www.sevenstories.com/pg/resources-academics or email academic@sevenstories.com.

Printed in the United States of America

9 8 7 6 5 4 3 2 1

For Roselia Marcial,
Julián in Cuba,
and in memory of Víctor García Domínguez:
my three teachers.

When you look into a pool of water or a mirror, the one you see there is not you and is not human.

—The words of an Angan speaker from Papua New Guinea, reported by Roy Wagner

Whose body would we have loved infinitely?

—Salvador Elizondo, *Farabeuf*

One need not be a Chamber—to be Haunted—
One need not be a House—
The Brain has Corridors—surpassing
Material Place—

—Emily Dickinson, "LXIX"

TRANSLATOR'S NOTE

As the daughter of immigrant parents, much of what I know of my Irish cultural heritage derives not from personal experience or books but from the stories I have been told throughout my life; stories related by family members and acquaintances or heard in songs, where the music provides an added element to the telling. These oral histories are often rich in detail and, as might be expected, change with the storyteller and their ability or desire to elaborate on the basic plot; when it came to my maternal aunt Creena, for instance, the elaboration knew few limits. It has often seemed to me that the truth-value of such stories is their least important aspect; their beauty lies in the telling and the listening, in what the storyteller wishes to recount and what the listener takes from it. And as the story migrates from place to place, from generation to generation, it metamorphoses, shape-shifts, speaks in other tongues, other voices.

When I first read Clyo Mendoza's novel *Fury* in Spanish it was this element of oral history that galvanized my attention. I delighted in the voices, the way they changed depending on the audience, the different versions they told in relation to who was or wasn't listening. Those voices filled my head, sang to me, and in my readings I felt like I was being carried along by their music, swept along by their tales, unconcerned that their accounts might vary. For me, Mendoza is a consummate storyteller, and like all of her kind, she knows how to enthral her audience.

Such thoughts naturally brought to mind Walter Benjamin's essay "The Storyteller."* And in this respect, I have the audacity to disagree with that great theorist to some extent. In this text, Benjamin draws a parallel between the decline of the storyteller and the associated role of the listener and the rise of the novel in its printed format. The reader of a novel is isolated, he writes, whereas someone "listening to a story is in the company of the storyteller." Storytellers weave personal or reported experience and make it "the experience of those who are listening to [the] tale."

Benjamin goes on to say, "All great storytellers have in common the freedom with which they move up and down the rungs of their experience as on a ladder." In my opinion, Clyo Mendoza fits within this definition. Where I begin to disagree with Benjamin is in his claim that the novel does not have its roots in the oral tradition. It seems to me that Mendoza has been a listener in this tradition, has crafted her work on that of other great storytellers, both renowned and anonymous, and offers us her own version of the story to make of what we will.

A translator has many, often competing tasks in the representation of an author's work in another language and culture. But on a personal level, when working on the translation of *Fury*, one of the most important of these was listening to the voices within the text, hearing the poetry and music contained there—it should come as no surprise that Clyo Mendoza is an

---

* Walter Benjamin, "The Storyteller: Reflections on the Works of Nikolai Leskóv," in *Illuminations*, trans. Harry Zohn (New York: Harcourt Brace Jovanovich, 1968), 83–109.

award-winning poet; there is nothing prosaic about her prose style. And the more attentively I listened, the clearer the voices became; in some strange, silent way they rang in my ears, occupied my head. All I had to do was write them down. Benjamin would claim that what is lost in the printed novel is the communal form of such listening, so that the experience becomes isolated, personal. And yet as a translator, that is diametrically opposed to my aim; I write for you to read, so you will also be attentive to those voices, will find them ringing in your ears, occupying your head. I am a storyteller offering you my version of the telling.

Perhaps what I am advocating here is for you read this novel—any novel—as a translator would, attentive to its voices and music; hearing them silently or sharing them aloud in your book clubs and reading groups, listening to them at author/translator events. For you to become the storyteller and the audience in a shared experience.

—Christina MacSweeney

I

The Notion of
the Body

Soldier One and Soldier Two met by a dead body whose open eyes reflected not the leaden wartime sky, but a light that gave a sense of blackness.

Soldier One and Soldier Two had approached the corpse, one to see if it belonged to a dead colleague, the other to check if his shot had hit its mark. The child's body glowed with the light that comes with death and his face was damp with the mist of all the evaporated blood. Fringing the bullet hole between his open eyes was a scab, formed immediately by the heat of the impact.

Soldier One and Soldier Two, still stupefied by the scene (as though it were the first death either of them had been involved in or witnessed), turned to look at each other, while the muzzles of their guns pointed in the same direction as their eyes, ready to fire.

There, in the midst of dead friends and enemies, neither Soldier One nor Soldier Two had any idea how the threat they posed to each other could be firmly communicated. They were horrified. And the fear one saw was seen by the other. That gaze, with death so close at hand, was communion. Without exchanging so much as a word, Soldier One gave himself up as a prisoner in order to escape from the battlefield, and it was only once they were standing on the lookout point from where the child had been shot that they began to talk.

Who were they? It was months since either of them had remembered that information. Orders had taken away their will and, without it, they had become killers, killing themselves at the same time.

The moon was waning, and under that crescent of light Soldier One and Soldier Two spoke their real names (I'm Lázaro; I'm Juan) and decided to desert.

They had to speak to the body before it would surrender. They said: Don't worry, just relax that jaw and stop frowning, it's all over. But the boy was still at war and rigor clenched the bones of his hands into fists. Let us dress you in white, little one, they said, loosen those fists. It was hours before they managed to get the boy's body to relax enough to show its palms. The lines of the right hand had been worn away by contact with his weapon and the left was covered in creases formed by holding on to nothingness. The hundreds of lines tracing out the horses that are said to indicate an early death led to the supposition that his fate had been predicted long before.

They were specialists in recovering fallen men and knew death was the only thing worth surrendering to. And so they sang the boy a lullaby to help him do just that. First the child's brow smoothed and they were able to remove the bullet. His fists opened, his jaws unclenched, and when he finally relaxed his whole body they dressed him in a white shirt.

Then they carried him away.

One of the men said that the sight of the boy had moved him so deeply that if it hadn't been for the hole, he'd have kissed his forehead.

When he was just one among the hordes of the war—like when he was walking at full tilt across the busiest street in the city and other humans brushed against his clothing, leaving a wake smelling of mouths, alcohol, and other unexpected things—he felt as if he were part of a machine, a tiny cog, like all the others. And even though thinking that made him feel insignificant, he also had the sense of being part of a whole. Maybe feeling this is God, he thought, but the first time his body fused with someone else's he had that same sensation; of boiling up next to another body until the two formed a single brew. The sweat helped, the mutual smearing of liquids when one entered the other or sometimes vice versa; because, in his case, he preferred bodies of his own sex. That was his great secret. He'd enlisted to clear his name, although no one knew just what he'd done wrong. His parents had always suspected; the way he moved one hand, the innate swinging of his hips made it clear he was an effeminate boy.

One day his father left, without him or his mother even noticing the absence for a while. The man was never around and his return was always well overdue. He was a travelling salesman in yarns. Not such badly paid work in those days when yarns were essential and weren't available in remote towns and villages; and a female clientele suited the womanizer perfectly.

The mother would say to her son: It's your fault he left. Deep down he knows that you want to be a girl. And, having had enough of her accusations, the son would reply with hurtful words: You're the guilty one, you're ugly, you never satisfied him in bed, you didn't give him what he had a right to. And so the bitterness and resentment grew with daily contact. Feathers flew and slaps resounded. He hit her too, more than once.

But even so, mother and son were inseparable. Circumstances demanded it, because when the war started the situation worsened. A lone female was easy prey and bandidos were carrying off widows and single women. They hassled the married women too, but there was a certain code of honor in battle between the men that made the wives slightly less accessible. And that was linked to another reason for enlisting, because a soldier was something "more than a man." And the crew cut fooled people who didn't know him. He tied his hands and hips with an imaginary thread, worked at roughening his voice, standing up straighter, and ridiculing the men with whom he had most in common. His mother wasn't proud of him, she said: Stay, child. Better we die together, don't leave me here on my own. But bitterness was already a dense, impenetrable mass of a monster. He told her he'd be back, set a cold kiss on her forehead, and went off to fight a war in which he had no idea who or what he was defending, or why.

Lázaro explained all that in the tumbledown building from which the boy had been killed, while Juan, listening in astonishment, recalled for the first time in many years his own life.

Passing themselves off as two brothers, a pair of muleteers, Lázaro and Juan rode through the desert, away from anyone who might recognize them. Their masculine clothing gave no hint of what they did at night, or in daylight hours when they found some convenient, solitary spot. Not even the bird that came to hover every day at the opening to the cave where they lived—watching them one astride the other, as if they were galloping—had discovered anything contrary to the laws of nature. Their cries would startle it only enough to fly a short distance and, tinged in the yellow light of the sun, the bird would sink its beak into the hanging fruit. The white pulp had ripened well around the wounds left by the sun on those rare desert fruits, there was a particular flavor in the small folds of flesh separating the parts that were rotten from the healthy; the sweet taste of ripeness made them all the more exquisite.

The bird's slender tongue would protrude from its beak like a pistil. Tiny droplets of juice dampened its breast and, having had its fill, it would fly high enough to be able to view the splendor of the sun on the empty road.

The sun stirred the animals.

Cicadas chirped, a frog freed the air trapped in its bulbous neck, dripping water murmured a damp psalm, horses shook themselves to scare off the flies and then moved in search of shade.

It was during those days of sun and fruit that Juan and Lázaro bought an old cart from a farmer, who told them it was the size of two coffins.

An elderly trader they came across, standing in the middle of the road next to a mule that had died of thirst, told them the story of a man from a nearby town who had sold his soul to the Devil in return for "the whole truth." The trader sprang onto the cart and began his tale without further ado: That man had been obsessed with the idea that his son had in fact been fathered by a neighbor. Before signing the contract, the Devil had told him that lies sometimes made life less burdensome, but the man, thinking that was the kind of thing the Devil, in his infinite evil, would say, and assuming the truth would free him of his obsession, decided to hurry along and sign the contract. Are you certain? asked the Devil, who was a very elegantly dressed man with a hat and shiny black shoes that never got dirty. I don't need your soul, he said, I already have many disciples who come to me of their own accord; I don't understand why you'd want to hand over half your life to me for a piece of foolishness. But if you insist, sign here with your blood and the deal is done.

The man signed as if the act would bring him a great fortune. At heart he didn't really believe the other was the Devil. Perhaps he signed the contract with such good grace because he doubted the efficacy of that well-dressed man who'd appeared at the crossroads, doubted that he was in fact who he claimed to be.

Killing himself laughing, the Devil handed the man a gold coin, saying it would bring him luck and warning him never to sell it.

Then he whispered "the whole truth" in his ear: the young boy wasn't his son and the woman wasn't his wife. He wasn't even a man; he was a dog. He'd been a poor, maddened creature cursed with bad dreams, even when he was awake. His visions had made him regress to a savage state; he growled during the day and howled at night.

When the man remembered his true body, he also remembered his suffering and became himself again. He was caged, chained, naked. Another man was looking into his eyes and witnessed the exact moment when the spark of understanding appeared in the animal's.

The other man was a sensation seeker, said the trader. A curious person who'd gone to take a look at the savage man. And he paid dearly for his curiosity because, when he looked into his eyes, the curse fell on him too, and after living almost his whole life on two legs, he too found himself running on all fours, tugging on his chain until the bones in his neck cracked.

The trader finished off his story with a totally unrelated comment. Laughing to himself, he said: It's ridiculous the way people always believe the Devil is elegantly dressed.

With a cry of, This is where I get off, the trader gave Juan and Lázaro a gold coin, informing them that it was very old and would bring good luck. Then he jumped from the cart.

Just like in the story, they said. And, roaring with laughter, the trader walked away, disappearing into nowhere.

Do you remember that boy you killed?

Juan made no response.

Juan, I'm talking to you.

You're drunk, Lázaro. Leave me in peace.

Well, I remember, Juan. You got him right between the eyes . . .

Oh shut it, you drunken sod.

Do you want to know what he was called?

Shut it! You're drunk, just shut up or you'll feel my knuckles in your face.

Lázaro crooned some incomprehensible song. His lips were sticking together and a thick film of white spittle was drying at the corners of his mouth.

He joined up for the love of a woman—or that's what he told us—but one day I saw him eying my dick . . .

In a flash, a fist smashed into his mouth and a soft groan, more like a prayer, was dragged unwillingly from his body.

I told you to shut it. Look what you've made me do, look what's happened . . .

Bloodstained spittle trickled from Lázaro's mouth and quickly soaked into the earth. Juan snuggled up against him and, holding his head so he wouldn't swallow, whispered: You're a drunken sod and I hate you.

Lázaro turned his eyes up as if he were trying to see into the darkness inside his skull. Juan was scared; he shook him until the pupils returned to the center of his eyeballs, focused. When he felt Lázaro's eyes turn to him with a glass-sharp gaze, Juan spoke again.

We're damned. You and I are damned for what we've done.

On hearing those words, Lázaro closed his eyes again and fell asleep.

I wish you'd tell me about yourself, Juan. Tell me something to help me sleep. Something about when you were a boy, about the person you were before the war, thought Lázaro as he stared at the other.

What are you looking at? asked Juan. Go to sleep.

I've got a bad feeling, like God's looking down on us. Haven't you ever asked yourself, Juan? Maybe it's true that we're sinning, and what's coming after this war will be even worse. I've had enough of killing, even the smell of meat makes me retch; it tastes of the fear of the animals we hunt, thought Lázaro, his eyes still fixed on Juan.

What's wrong with you, Lázaro? Stop looking at me that way, you don't let me get any rest.

Juan turned over, showing a back covered in scratches, scars, and rope marks. He stood up, blew out the candle. When he finally fell asleep, Lázaro was still awake.

That night, Lázaro had the sense of being a child again, in the darkness of the cave it was impossible to see your hands. He felt as though he'd shrunk, was very small, that if he tried to get to his feet, his bones wouldn't be able to bear the weight of his body and he'd fall.

I've got a bad feeling, Juan, a bad feeling, he murmured. Juan had been his only audience for a long time. Even when he talked to himself, the listener bore that name.

The night stretched out and he was shrinking. I'm going to disappear, he told himself. A sense of relief replaced his fright. And then he realized that for a few moments he'd forgotten about Juan, and a terrible feeling of guilt, like a weight, began to sour the air in his lungs. I can't leave without him, I can't just vanish, he told himself again, and so the night passed. One vision followed another: Juan's body turned into a dying animal, Juan's body was a huge mass, Juan's body merged into the darkness of the cave and the density of his flesh made the air heavy.

The ambulant trader told them about a girl who was in the habit of throwing herself on women and biting them, and her saliva awakened in them the desire for others of their own sex. He told them that the first time she bit a woman, her victim said she'd felt her heart changing: she was following the long tresses, guided by a scent that only she could smell. She was like a dog lost among women until one took her hand and led her away. Once, an old blind lady carried her off and didn't bring her back that day.

When she returned, the girl said that, despite her blindness, the lady could find her way around perfectly: she'd taken her to a bedroom where the blankets were edged with very fine needle lace, unbuttoned her blouse and started to nibble and suck on her breasts until a clear milk oozed from them and ran down her stomach to her crotch.

The blind lady kneaded her breasts, took the milk in her hands and filled her eyes with it, moaning all the while. The girl said that, almost in a flash, the woman turned into a man and lifted her skirt to reveal a penis pointing straight up. She said this man thrust the penis between her legs and, when he entered her, she clearly felt the moment she conceived.

She was pregnant on her return, and when she told her story, her family took her far into the desert and abandoned her there, so she would never come back to shame them.

Where do you get those stories from? Juan asked the trader, who had appeared out of nowhere that day and, without even the excuse of a dead mule, had sprung onto the cart; he seemed to have been waiting for them at the same spot in the road.

A little bird told me them, he said with a laugh.

After the notion of death had returned to Juan's mind, irritated by the violent course his thoughts were taking, he sought out Lázaro and said: I wish you were a woman. That way I'd feel like a regular man. Then he moved away to stare into the fire, thinking about the men who, according to him, lived there and were—had to be—human scars. Lázaro did nothing. Lázaro said nothing. Sometimes he'd pass whole days in silence, but on this occasion he finally opened his mouth to say: I dreamed of my father, Juan, and this time he didn't beat me; he was crouching in the corner of a house, like a scared child. I went to him to see what the problem was, but when I managed to tug his hands from his face he looked at me as if he'd seen the Devil. He screamed, and his scream was shrill. Words issued from his foaming mouth. I don't remember the rest of the dream, but I've got the feeling that something is wrong. I'm really afraid. I've never been this afraid, not even in the war.

Suddenly another voice interrupted Lázaro.

There was the trader again, at the entrance to the cave, holding a lantern. Hello, boys, he said. I've been looking for you.

Juan always had his fists at the ready when he was frightened. The trader said: I've come to tell you a story. It's the story of a man who sold yarn in the mountains and, while on his rounds, he fucked a few widows. There are lots of single women around here and all the men are away at war. Or they were, isn't that right? Allow me to tell you this pretty story.

The trader came into the cave and, in his fright, Juan moved to punch him but the trader's body instantly vanished into the shadows.

Lázaro's eyelids drooped and when he opened them again he saw Juan still staring into the flames. He was counting the men who lived in the firelight. When he noticed that Lázaro had woken, he said: You were having a nightmare, I couldn't sleep for your screams. I'll never be able to get a moment's rest until you're dead. Isn't that so?

He rubbed his hands. They were stained black.

What happened to your hands? asked Lázaro.

I was fiddling with the ashes, he replied.

Afterwards, their dicks looked at one other with those small eyes oozing their white liquid. And they looked at each other with their upper eyes too, their dark, almond-shaped eyes.

If only the two of us were a single man, Juan would say when he was drunk, we'd be more macho than anyone else; even the way we are, we used to put fear into the hearts of the other recruits. Lázaro laughed. Darling, he said, from a bird's-eye view you really are a young lady. And he walked off, swinging his naked hips. Juan caught up with him, spun him around, and slapped his face. Don't ever say that again, Lázaro. You might find it hard to believe, but we're men. Well, Lázaro retorted as he mounted his horse, what difference does it make whether we're sods, men, or women: no one cares, for God's sake; we're nobody, Juan.

Juan watched him go, his right hand throbbing from the slap. He'll come back, he told himself. He can't go far.

But by the time the light was fading, Lázaro still hadn't returned.

The next day, under a sun so strong it bleached the color from the wings of the birds, an insistent anxiety was drilling in Juan's head. He mounted his horse and set out across the plain until the mountains began to turn blue and the cold was cutting him to the bone.

A small herd of wild horses brought the smell of grass and an animal scent to his nostrils. Lázaro's horse was galloping behind them. Juan managed to lasso it. Where did Lázaro go, beast? he asked, but there was no reply. He was afraid to approach the town, was afraid of bandidos, and, deep down, was afraid of all men.

He didn't initially call out, but after saying Lázaro's name, the shout issued from his mouth and was carried on the wind to a goatherd. She followed the desperate cry and found Juan still mounted on his horse.

Who are you looking for?

My brother.

Is he a man about this tall with a scar on his face?

Yes, that will be him. Juan felt as if he were going to topple from his horse and die there and then.

We found a man like that.

Is he alive? he asked. And she said: Follow me.

They've found us, Juan, said Lázaro.

Someone told them that two men had come here; someone told them that since we were both men and enemies, we'd decided to team up. They say we're rebels, that we're planning to form a new squadron, that we're plotting. I galloped off when they saw me, but they know we're here, Juan. We have to leave.

Lázaro tried to get to his feet but some invisible force was pushing his head toward the ground. The fire of the clay stove reached out to where he was lying, casting its light on him.

Juan didn't know whether Lázaro's story was true or the product of his fevered imagination.

We found him lying in the road this morning, said the goatherd. My mother brought him here. She nodded toward a corner of the room where a hunched woman was staring into the fire. Your brother was very nearly dead, it was so cold last night. We didn't know what to do, but you don't leave a good soul to die alone in the middle of nowhere.

The girl approached to press a damp cloth to Lázaro's lips. Your brother's burning up with fever, lad. Take him with you, we can't be responsible for him. We don't want any more dead men in this house.

Juan strapped Lázaro to his horse and offered his thanks. The old woman turned to him just at the moment when one log fell on another, making a few embers fly into the air. The fire blazed up, filling the old woman's toothless mouth with light. Juan believed she was smiling, but it could just as well have been the expression of someone whose features are set in a permanent scream. In the corner, the old woman raised her hand and stretched out a deeply lined palm in what might have been a farewell, but the hand stayed there, static, the gesture unfinished.

Juan thanked them once more, checked that Lázaro was firmly strapped to the horse, and galloped back to their hideaway.

Tell me who you saw, Lázaro. Who's found us? Where were they?

Lázaro wasn't looking at anyone, his eyes were turned up and his tongue was coated in a pale substance. Please, tell me, Lázaro. Who did you meet that night? Lázaro, please, answer me, I'm begging you, look at me, say something, anything.

Flies were swarming around the cuts in the skin of the fruit.

Lázaro, I'm frightened. Can you try a little harder? You can't leave me here alone.

Do you remember when we were going to kill each other? Your gun was pointed at my chest and mine at yours. I swear I was going to kill you, but I was afraid. Frightened in just the way I am now. You can't leave me, do you hear? You're all I have, Lázaro.

Juan squeezed the juice of a fly-bitten fruit into Lázaro's mouth. It trickled over his tongue, darkening for a few seconds the white mass accumulating there due to his feverish thirst. He was burning up: Juan could feel the heat when he put his hand close to Lázaro's body. You're going to die on me, he said. And then what will I do?

The idea of death grew within him like something akin to the long desert horizon. A great, black, cubic space, something his eyes were incapable of measuring. He didn't understand how all that sorrow could fit inside him. It was as though, in order to accommodate so much pain, his body had turned itself inside out. He felt as if his whole being had been inverted, that his internal organs were exposed. That his body and his sorrow comprised everything, except what it was before Lázaro's death.

The flies buzzed around the cuts in the skin of the fruit, they flew into things, their sticky feet started to land on the body of the sick man.

Juan kneeled beside Lázaro again.

Please, listen to me, you have to hold out a little longer. I can't go for help if they're looking for us and, anyway, I wouldn't have any idea who to ask. We're alone, we don't know anyone. Please, Lázaro, hold out a little longer. Tell me something, go on, tell me something so you don't fall asleep.

The flies came closer to Juan's face, mistaking his tears for water, they collided with the wounded hands of those two men, with the bodies of the horses, with other flies.

Juan, said Lázaro.

A few disjointed words began to emerge from his lips. Somewhere water was dripping.

Juan, Lázaro said again. I'm so afraid, Juan. They're coming for us, the dark shadows are coming for us.

And that was how Lázaro used his last breath: They're coming for us, the dark shadows are coming for us. Hold me, I'm frightened. Who's this woman? Are the shadows after her too? Juan, they're after me, it's cold.

The flies confused the white area between his eyelids with the cuts in the skin of the fruit.

It was a shame that one died just when I was feeding it . . .

My mother's telling that story again, thought Lázaro. She was talking about the puppies they rescued. His mother fed them goat's milk from her little finger. Poor creatures, she said to her friends (they were sitting around her, their backs to Lázaro), I thought I could save them, even if they were crawling with maggots. Everyone said it wasn't worth the effort.

But they were with me for five days, five days those puppies lasted. There was a reason why the bitch abandoned them, everyone said. But I really did believe I was going to save them. At night I soaked pieces of bread, gave them more milk. I filled small bowls with hot water and laid them beside the puppies so they'd think their mother was there. And though to tell the truth we never have milk in the house, you have to do the best you can for the little ones. Isn't that so, Lázaro?

Lázaro had the sensation that something wasn't quite right.

Isn't that so, Lázaro? You have to do the best you can. Lázaro, are you listening to me? Lázaro?

Lázaro couldn't see his mother properly. It was as if a drop of milk had entered each of his eyes, a white mist was spreading across his irises.

Aren't I right, child? A drop of the milk of a woman who's just given birth can return the sight to the blind. Child? Lázaro, are you listening to me?

The women sitting around his mother turned to look at Lázaro. They had no eyes. They opened their mouths and had no teeth.

Lázaro, are you listening to me? Hold out, Lázaro. Don't leave me here.

Lázaro remembered a man, a man who was pointing a gun at his chest, a man looking at him in horror. Who was that man? What was he doing there?

Mother, said Lázaro, I can't see you. I can only see a man. Who is he, Mother?

Everything I know of you comes from your stories about other people. You've never said: This happened to me. You tell an anecdote about someone else, never mentioning yourself. But I recognize you in all those stories. When you're talking to me, I feel that you've always been a shadow in your own life, like a spy observing all the people in your life before I came into it. And they are ghosts. People you loved, people I'll never know.

You've never told me your first memory, but I feel I really know the things you only talk about to me. You're good at telling things, Juan. I always believe whatever you say. And if I haven't wanted to tell you much about myself either, it's just been a matter of following your lead, and maybe that's why we've been happy, if you can call the thing that sprung up between us in those days of hunger and war happiness. We wandered for years in search of paths where there was no revolution besides the one in our own heads, and in the end the best place for us was the desert. But war reached here too. Maybe love isn't enough, Juan: it can't win out over death, for instance. Whose side am I on now? In the squadron we were always arguing about who suited us best. By the time I met you, I didn't know which country I belonged to, didn't know what true justice was, didn't even know how the damn war started. Now I don't know if it's finished or who won it. We've been real men because we've always been fighting. Isn't that what real men are meant to do? We've done that part. And so far we've won through, because we aren't dead. But I can't take any more. I'm begging you to go away and leave me here. There's no hope for me. Take a good look at me, I know you can see that what's coming next is my death. I'm not sad, Juan. I swear to you there's no need for that. I've been happy, even though I come from a line of people where everyone died bemoaning their fate. I've had a companion in this world during these times when the smoke of war has been in our eyes, it's damaged our heads, our brains no longer allow us to imagine the future. I don't need a brain, Juan, I swear I don't. I feel I'm getting lighter. Soon I'll be gone and I want you to know that, in spite of the suffering, life has been good to me. You've been good to me. Go away and leave me here. Take the road to Las Ánimas, over yonder, where you can see the dam, and go straight on, don't stop. There used to be a dry stone wall alongside the road. Follow it. At some point, you'll come to my mother's house. Break the lock, if it's still there. Things here die more peacefully, but metal rusts fast. All you'll need is a long nail and a rock. I don't think anyone will have been in there because the house is cursed and they're all scared of it. If anyone ever dared to break the lock, my mother would stick it back together with her dead-woman's spittle. They'd have taken to their heels before discovering the treasure in there. I know my mother hid that coin somewhere, Juan. Maybe under the altar to the Virgin or in a hole. Smash all her statues of saints if you have to, because the coin might be inside one of them. And when you find it, put it in your pocket and leave. I can't go on any longer, I'm tired, so tired. My mother was keeping that coin for my future bride, that was what she used to tell me. The old girl always wanted a grandson and she wanted the mother of that nonexistent child to treasure a gold coin for her whole life. The old girl didn't even sell it when she had nothing to eat.

Take it, Juan, you're my wife.

Juan watched Lázaro's mouth moving but no words came out. He was struggling to speak, there was sweat on his brow. The light of the candle glistened in those droplets, the flame moved about as if it had bones. Lázaro's temperature was way too high. Hold out a little longer, said Juan, tomorrow we'll ride off together and we'll find something. He tried to dampen the dry lips with a bitter nopal, but Lázaro's white tongue went limp and his eyes turned inwards.

When Lázaro dies, Juan flies into a rage, hammering his fists against the rocks. After a few minutes of this, with his knuckles raw, it occurs to him that he might need them to fight someone. If Lázaro died with the truth on his lips, then he would, and it was a serious mistake to have left those knuckles on the rocks. If what Lázaro said before his death were correct, he'd have to fight. The two enemy bands would unite with the sole intention of torturing him. Once the dog is dead, the mange is gone, as the saying goes. He imagines them tying the top half of his body to the torso of a horse, with the bottom half on a crazed mule, dying to run off to sate its hunger on the sparse blades of green grass in the shade of the rocks. He imagines fire on the soles of his feet, stone slabs cracking his ribs, blunt knives clumsily amputating body parts. A penis hitting the ground with the dull plop of a sickly bird falling from the nest. Juan decides that he has to go away. For better or worse, he has to go.

The decision made, his mind turns to practical matters.

As if nothing he does is real, or is a macabre dance, he wraps Lázaro in a blanket. So the animals won't get to his body too soon, he tells himself. He counts the coins, packs his things, and takes enough water to see him through the journey without stopping. There's the sound of dripping coming from somewhere. He carries an oil lamp to the back of the cave, where

Lázaro had stowed some knapsacks. Time to put everything on the fire, to cover his tracks. He finds a couple of flour sacks he hasn't seen before. Inside are papers, some odds and ends, a few envelopes.

Make a choice, Juan, throw the sacks on the fire or look inside them.

Juan is certain that in those sacks Lázaro kept what remained of his life before he became a soldier, before he became a deserter. A life in which Juan didn't yet figure. Curiosity gets the better of him, practicality vanishes. Hurry, Juan, he tells himself, but the voice in his mind is music without a tune; there are too many questions inside his head. Who did Lázaro love before me? Would there be some trace of him or them in the sacks? Was he thinking of someone else while he was coming with me? Juan's trying to soothe one pain with another. He's trying to hate Lázaro, to sink into bitterness, he's trying to make himself believe that he'd already been abandoned before Lázaro's death. He still feels that he deserves everything he's suffering, even if it happens outside his own body. Like those hares he used to slit from neck to tail, that would then curl open on contact with the fire, Juan still feels that his body has been turned inside out. If he were to find some indication in the sacks that Lázaro wasn't who he said he was, then he'd be free and everything would return to its proper place. He'd just leave him there and ride off thinking: I've been wasting my time.

Juan opens one of the sacks.

Some photographs. A few letters. A map. The damp atmosphere of the cave has made the photos stick together, it isn't easy to separate them.

Further back, the dripping finally stops, that water will be suspended in the darkness for eons; centuries, millions of years after Juan and Lázaro, it will be turned to stone.

Hearing the sound of water dripping, a bird flies into the cave, guided by the light from the lantern Juan is holding. Its wings flap so quickly, so close to him, that Juan starts in surprise and the photographs fall onto his muddy boots. He doesn't pick them up. He looks at the letters but doesn't read them. He doesn't know how. He's ashamed to think that Lázaro could. How did he learn? Who was Lázaro before becoming his Lázaro? His shame ebbs and he hurriedly gathers up the photos. The one on his left boot shows a woman sitting on a couch, the backcloth of a sky behind her. Juan peels a second photo from behind the first: the same woman, this time with a child on her lap. A man dressed in a suit but wearing sandals stands with a hand resting on the seated woman's shoulder. His face can't be seen, not because the damp has blurred it: someone has scratched out the features with a coin or their fingernail.

Questions are lining up. It's hard for Juan to decide if the child in the photo is Lázaro. He's plump, barefoot, and dressed in a smock with a lace collar. It isn't Lázaro's scarred, bearded face with those questioning eyes. What's the point of life if you're always afraid of yourself? he'd once asked and Juan had mocked him (Lázaro, what kind of dumb question is that?), but he was unable to sleep for asking himself the very same question. Lázaro never minded having, as he put it, a woman inside him. He delighted in being himself in the cave, dancing to the music of dripping water and the strange sound he made by clicking his tongue on the roof of his mouth.

Which one was Lázaro in that photograph? Had he at some time fathered a child and loved a woman? Juan didn't believe it. Anyway, Lázaro could just as easily be the woman: not the child, not the man with the scratched-out face. Neither of them, it wasn't possible.

On the ground, to one side of his boot, Juan sees another photo. He quickly stoops to pick it up.

He sees the same man, but with his face intact. The child has grown and the woman isn't in the shot. The man reminds him of someone. Who? It isn't Lázaro, but if not, where does he know him from?

The heavy hand on the child's shoulder makes him lean slightly to his left. That stance, something the photographer couldn't have foreseen at the moment of clicking the shutter, is what helps him to recognize the child as Lázaro. Whenever someone made him feel uncomfortable, his body would try to distance itself from them by tilting to one side. Juan had always thought it was a hangover from childhood. And here was the proof: on the back of the photo, in fading but beautiful cursive writing, it said that Lázaro was six.

My father used to sell yarns around the place where you were born, Lázaro had once told Juan. Imagine if my father had known you when you were a child, before I came along. Imagine if my father had sold your mother threads to sew your clothes. That was the only time Lázaro had mentioned his father. He'd been drunk and was playfully passing his hands over the fire as he spoke. He moved them so quickly that the flow of air prevented those hands from being burned. Look, Juan, I'm a sorcerer, he said. The firelight glowed at his feet, casting flickering shadows onto the walls of the cave.

When Lázaro was a child and his mother used to lead him by the hand to the cemetery, the sand would burn his legs, each step sending up sizzling sparks that stung his calves and thighs.

The desert stretched out alongside the dead, and in the cemetery there was nothing more than stones and a few blades of grass; only the earth took nourishment from the corpses. Lázaro and his mother brought flowers; just a few, but still quite fresh. And that particular day some men were singing dirges in their own language as they wove the palm fronds of the only awning that offered shade in the cemetery. They didn't turn to watch Lázaro and his mother enter because there was no gate; the cemetery was in fact just a collection of crosses with no fence, capable of expanding on all sides, but small, as the town had always been.

The man never looked at them; they kept their faces close to the palm fronds, as if they were smelling them. Their hats were pulled down over their ears, and only their black hands emerging from the sleeves of their long white smocks were visible, the fingers braiding, braiding very quickly.

The mother moved to the shade of the awning. She was so tall—or that's how Lázaro remembered her—she almost reached the sky and even higher up were the men, who went on singing their dirges. Lázaro didn't understood what they were singing because he'd never learned his mother's native tongue. She walked along, very serious, listening carefully, and stopped at the grave of Cástula, the girl who'd died unwed.

Lázaro looked down because his legs were itching and he thought it must be ants. And then came the silence. The desert silence, crossing the whole plain unhindered. Lázaro raised his eyes in search of the men on the awning but they'd gone. There was no one there except his mother, talking to the flowers, and to Cástula.

He said: Mom, I looked up but couldn't see the men who were singing.

Silence followed, not even the wind made any noise.

His mother spoke: I'll tell you something, but don't be startled, Lazarito. Those men you saw were the dead constructing a shadow.

When they left the cemetery it was already dark. Lázaro couldn't remember if they had gone there at the hour of the siriama—when you can watch the sun go down and the sky tinge a reddish gold—or if they had spent hours singing to Cástula that afternoon.

His mother liked singing to the girl.

Cástula and his mother had never, as far as was known, been close. Everyone in town, including his mother, said that Cástula was mad, and they were afraid of her. Years after the day at the cemetery and the dead men, Lázaro heard rumors that his mother had made a promise to that girl who, despite her youth, seemed like an old woman. The promise was that if she—the girl—agreed to keep a secret and died before his mother, she'd go to sing to her every day. Nobody ever knew what that secret was because Cástula took it with her to the grave. Lázaro was by then looking for a reason to get away from his mother and when the rumor reached his ears, something told him that he'd been handed that reason on a plate, his perfect excuse. He decided to solve the mystery as there was no doubt that whatever Cástula had been hiding concerned him: he was almost the only thing his mother had any association with.

Essentially predictable, everlastingly naive, his mother had secreted a few envelopes in the false back of a drawer. Lázaro read the letters contained there. For several years, he and his mother had been taught to read and write by a very old foreign woman who had come to live in the desert on some unrevealed, personal mission. His mother paid for the lessons with food and water. And that was how Lázaro was able to read the letters. They were short, unsigned, and not easily understood:

Yesterday I saw Vicente. He was walking along holding the hand of a young girl and he kissed her as if she were a woman, I think they live in Boca de Perro. He isn't dead, he hasn't gone to the war, the swine just walked out on you.

I can't do what you ask because it's against God's will. If you want him dead so badly, come here and kill him yourself. A few coins are no exchange for an eternity in hell.

I believe they had a child. I'll write his address below. I can't do any more for you. Don't write to me again. Think about what you're planning, Sara. God has his punishments.

The only thing he'd have preferred to avoid was the thirst that plagued him before his death. It made him think of when he'd arrived in Boca de Perro and hurried in search of water; he knocked and kicked on doors, pleaded, but no one in the town opened up. The thirst made his mind go over and over the same ideas: when people die you have to wait nine days before burying them so their souls recover from the fright and leave their bodies, so they don't get confused, lost. Nine days, that's the exact length of time.

Thirst always reminded him of the war. He began talking to himself: You have to put all the bodies in a pit as soon as possible, almost immediately.

He recalled the pits in the desert that aren't visible because they are full. Full of people, of bones the breeze sometimes unearths and that animals chew on to clean their teeth.

I killed men too. And women. And children. I wanted honor. I wanted to eat. I wanted to find my father, Lázaro says to himself. They'd told me that he was a soldier and had gone to fight in the war, but one day I found some letters, and in them a woman called Cástula told my mother that he'd never enlisted: he was living with another family in a town called Boca de Perro, far from where I was born. By the time I found that out, it was already too late: I'd joined the army. But I decided that before I died in a war that changed its name but never ended, I had to set eyes on that man my mother never forgot.

Boca de Perro was a miserable, dusty town full of ailing people. After a long, hot journey, I finally managed to get there, but was very thirsty, so the first thing I did was to look for water. Everyone had warned me not to taste a drop of the water in that town because it was cursed and whoever drank it would never leave. A pack of lies, right? Old people will make up anything just for the fun of it. I was parched, but there wasn't a single tree looking more or less alive to indicate that there was water nearby. Then I spotted a garden in the middle of a plot of land that was just dust, a garden with roses and mango trees. I ran toward it to pick some fruit, tried to climb a tree from the barrel cactus fence, but that plant uses its spines as protection and when I was almost there, the branch I was on broke and I fell onto them. A girl dashed out from the house with a garden and instead of scolding, she looked at me in pity and pulled the spines from my flesh while I ate a mango, a few nopals, and drank a lot of water. She was very pretty, like those northern girls with their wide-set eyes and thick lashes. Her long, jet-black hair was braided. What are you doing here, son? she asked. I didn't understand why the young woman would talk as if she were older than me. Before I could reply, I heard a child crying and she immediately went back into the house. She returned with him in her arms and, covering herself with a shawl, began to feed him. He was old to be still at the breast.

I listened to his snuffling, the way he stopped sucking so as not to choke on the milk; I looked on as damp stains began to appear on the mother's dress. His father's there inside, she said with a fearful look, nervously covering herself. The way I was watching made her uneasy, but I've never liked women, I was just looking at the child, a little jealous of how he was being treated. I got down to business: I'm searching for a man, maybe you know him, he's called Vicente Barrera. He lives here, said the woman. I wasn't expecting that. My knees turned to jelly. I asked her to let me see my father, but without admitting that's who he was. She replied: That won't be possible, what do you want with him? You've heard what they say around here, haven't you? But get one thing straight right away: my husband isn't a circus animal, son, so do me the favor of leaving. Then she removed the child from her breast and went on: Look what you've done, my milk's souring. Go now. But I didn't. I lied to that woman, saying Vicente had been a close friend of my father, that I wanted to hear a story to remember him by, and that was why I'd come so far to find her husband. They were friends in the other war. A little perplexed, the girl looked at me and, with a thoughtful expression, said: So Vicente really was a soldier. I didn't understand what she was talking about and just nodded. Then I told her that my father had left my mother and me to fight and that I'd scarcely known him, but wanted to hear about him. I shed a few tears, and they weren't feigned, because deep down I'd believed that story, even though I was there, staring the truth in the face, and my father was a son of a bitch who'd left us for another woman. The girl's heart softened and she said: My husband may not be in a condition to tell you anything. I asked why and she replied: Come inside and see for yourself.

There, in a darkened room constructed of earth and mule dung, was my father. We crept in, so as not to wake him, I guess. The girl lit a candle. A flame is the only thing that doesn't hurt his eyes, she said. And then I recognized the old man: the graying hair, the scarred face, the rigid, stick-dry body. His hands and feet were bound. Why do you keep him tied up? I shouted at the girl. She responded with a sob: He's mad.

The old man opened his eyes. He saw me and began to growl like a rabid animal. He foamed at the mouth, bit his tongue and bloodstained spittle drooled from his jaws. So I left without saying a word. I didn't spit in his face, didn't make demands on him. I said: Thanks for the fruit and the water, ma'am. And then I turned as she locked the door, crying and saying in an almost inaudible voice: My milk's going to sour, my milk's going to sour.

II
Anatomy of
the Shadow

Before her death, Cástula was driven mad by her ghosts. She'd always been on the move, fleeing the war only to arrive by chance at places where the most awful battles were being unleashed. So fleeing once more, she'd returned to seek refuge in her hometown, where no one now remained and no one told her that the war was over.

She returned when she began to feel death close at hand and decided that she wanted to end her life in the place where she'd been born, as if that were, in some way, an unraveling of the enormous skein in which she'd gotten tangled.

Although still young, Cástula seemed very old. It was said she'd once done something unpardonable and that was why she'd lost her bloom. She looked like a wrinkled fruit.

Cástula's skin was so black she could spy on lovers in the dark without being seen. You're really getting turned on, aren't you, Rosita? said a young man sucking on his girl's nipple, but she replied: I thought it was you breathing so heavily.

The whites of Cástula's eyes disappeared into the night and the distant sound of a door banging was heard.

The same thing happened to many other couples, but no one could be certain that it was Cástula, "the girl who died unwed."

They all thought she departed life without being touched by a man because she'd been away from the town for many years, and as nothing ever happened there, people believed that those who left remained as they had been. Yet in fact Cástula was always hounded by war.

The first time she left, fleeing from the soldiers, she was walking along one pleasant afternoon, trying to look at the sun without closing her eyes, when a man on horseback carried her off. He let her go, but she was pregnant.

Cástula gave birth to a boy. She detested the man but loved the child, so she never complained. At least not until war caught up with her again.

Cástula finally recovered consciousness two days after the bandidos had entered. They had left her with wounds all over her body, but still alive. Crushed by grief, she found her child on the floor. He'd died of hunger.

That may be why Cástula began to feel so much love for little Lázaro, the son of her neighbor, Sara. One day, Sara found her suckling the child and took him from her arms, calling her a dirty pig. Sara had a rough tongue; she was deeply unhappy because she'd fallen in love with an itinerant seller of yarns and he'd left her. So she tended to take things out on Cástula. She used to yank her braids to make them come loose, but afterwards she'd allow her to breastfeed Lázaro and would re-braid the long hair. It's said they were sometimes seen bathing together, one of them washing the other's breasts with soapwort, and then they seemed to be suckling each other. In the town it was rumored that Sara asked a favor of Cástula: she sent her to sell some goats in another town, where she'd been told that her husband—Vicente, the yarn salesman—was stationed. Word had come to her that he was now an honorable soldier, dedicated to killing the enemy and with no time to visit his family, but she hadn't believed it.

Cástula set out.

Although she had a reputation for chastity in the town, once away, she slept with a few soldiers, hoping to help Sara, but none of them had heard of Vicente Barrera. Then one day, as she was walking across the town square, a very dirty woman, who until a moment before seemed to have been leaning against a wall sleeping, lunged at her legs and bit and bit until someone pulled her off and tied her to a tree. And there they left the woman, growling, until she fell asleep on her feet again.

Cástula told the children that she'd begun to prefer women from that very moment and so, when she was found with her hand up someone's skirt, it was all the fault of the woman who had bitten her.

Soon everyone in the town she'd reached knew she was a very odd young woman and after they had kicked her out and she was walking, defeated, back to Sara, a bejeweled woman stopped her in the dark. Get up onto my horse, she said, and Cástula jumped up behind her.

In the darkness of the house, Cástula sensed the opulence of the furniture. The only lighting was a single candle carried by the woman. A silk bedspread gleamed when the droplet of fire passed close by.

Who are you? asked Cástula as the woman parted her legs and examined her sex as if it were a rose. Without replying, the woman put Cástula's hand into her mouth. Then she said: Your skin, negrita, feels like the skin of a mango.

Cástula recounted that the woman then suddenly took hold of her breasts and squeezed them until the milk she used to feed to Lazarito began to appear. She said she couldn't stop it and that, in the dribble of light from the candle, she was able to make out the woman drinking the milk and putting it in her eyes. I'm blind, the woman told her between moans, mother's milk cures blindness. And when she spoke, Cástula could see that there were no teeth in the woman's mouth. She bit her hard with her toothless gums and the milk trickled down to their thighs. Look what I have here, said the blind woman, and moving the candle to the dark triangle of her pubis and searching there as if the mass of hair were a thicket of shrubs, she extracted a small penis and stuck it into poor Cástula, who instantly felt that she was conceiving a child. So you are a man too, she sighed, as if the words pained her.

When Cástula returned to Sara, smiling and full of life, the first thing she did was to hold out her hands, displaying the money she'd obtained from the sale of the goats and the gold coin given to her by the blind woman.

It's for Lazarito, Sara.

Where did you get that?

A woman gave it to me.

Although her skin was very dark, Cástula's cheeks flushed deep red after Sara slapped her.

You're a dirty pig, Sara said, taking the coin, wrapping it in a piece of cloth, and hurrying to find a spade to dig a hole. Did you hear any news of Vicente? Cástula hung her head in shame or fear.

No, Sara.

You just went whoring, didn't you, Cástula? She dragged her away by the braids, with Lazarito watching the whole scene.

Take good note, Lázaro, said his mother, brushing hairs from her hands. Under this tree is the money that will save your life. Dig it up when you find a woman and have to give a dowry. When the war's over, this coin will give you the means to marry.

Cástula was standing in the doorway, her braids hanging loose.

I swear I'll find Vicente. When I've had my child, I'll be able to go anywhere you want.

You can't be pregnant, Cástula. That's just air in your belly.

As the months passed, Cástula grew fatter. Her breasts swelled and her belly protruded at the front and sides as though she were growing an adult man in there.

Sara took her to see the midwife.

That white-haired woman who welcomed the desert children into the world readied her hands, drew her fingers together like two arrowheads and then felt Cástula's belly with the fleshy part of her palms. She searched and searched the flesh but it seemed she could find nothing. I'm going to put my fingers inside, she said. Cástula sweated and pressed her lips tight as the woman tried to find the child. The old lady finally went to the basin and washed her hands, deep in thought. After looking into the water for a while, she beckoned Sara over.

There's no child inside Cástula, she said.

But what about her belly?

There's nothing in there, it's empty. That's what I'm saying.

She has milk coming from her breasts . . .

But there's nothing there, Sara. I'm certain. I don't know what Cástula's growing inside her, but a flesh and blood person it isn't.

Just what are you saying?

Cástula isn't pregnant, it's the same as happens to bitches when they want to have pups but aren't allowed. They swell up, their teats fill with milk, they lie on the ground looking up to the sky as if they really are expecting . . .

Like bitches.

Have pity on her, Sara dear. That child is very unhappy. She's gotten the idea that a baby is growing inside her; imagine how it will be when she finds it's never going to be born.

Sara left the woman on her knees. She shook out her skirt, turned to Cástula, who was still lying on the ground, staring into space, and said: Let's go.

She left a few pesos for the old woman, who took them and whispered in her ear: I'm pleading with you, Sarita. Have compassion for Cástula.

Sara didn't walk toward the house, but to the scrubland, and when she reached the edge of the town, she went on walking.

Sara, Lazarito is home alone. Where are we going?

Sara didn't reply.

Lazarito will be scared, Sara. Why don't we turn back?

Cástula was stroking her belly with her open palm and Sara watched her out of the corner of her eye in disgust. Sara, if I have a girl, can I call her after you?

Sara went on walking briskly without speaking.

In the dusk, on the great plain, the only sound was their breathing. Eyes glinted here and there between the bushes and a huge tumbleweed with pale branches was rolling along in the distance. That looks like a fat woman skipping, said Cástula, nervously stroking her belly. Can't we go back now? Where are you taking me? It isn't the full moon yet, Sara. We might get lost.

Sara still hadn't walked far enough and, anyway, she knew every inch of the path. Vicente had showed it to her; they used to sneak away there on nights like that one. It flashed across her mind that she'd gotten pregnant with Lázaro right there.

Cástula was singing, saying things to her belly, saying things to Sara, but Sara didn't answer.

At the dead of night, Sara held her breath and began walking slowly backwards. She hid behind an agave and Cástula continued on ahead.

What are you doing, Sara? I can't see you.

Sara said nothing. She didn't feel capable of saying anything, not a single word.

Cástula walked on and Sara listened as her voice faded in the distance.

It felt like playing a prank. It's just a game, she told herself, nothing but a game.

Sara, I'm frightened. Where are you? I'm stretching out my arm but you're not here at my side. I don't want to play anymore, said Cástula like a child on the verge of tears. Sara!

Sara had stayed back behind the agave, scarcely breathing.

Cástula has moved further away. She looks like a pink dress floating in the air, because her skin is so black, thought Sara. She's a black-skinned harlot.

Cástula's pink dress soon vanished. Sara waited a while longer and then, when there was no sound from the girl, she turned back, brushing against thorn bushes on her way home.

Time stretched out when the war was over, few soldiers had returned and the pivotal moment of any day was when those that did suffered nightmares in the marital bed.

On one of the days when Sara had dragged a chair over to the door and stayed there until nightfall, a letter arrived, and that was a great event. It announced the birth of Cástula's son. And, more specifically, it announced that Cástula had found Vicente, Sara's husband. Over two years had gone by and Sara had given her up for dead, but in her letter, even though it was short, Cástula sounded happy, lighthearted.

Sara asked for more information, she wrote line after line of congratulations on the birth of the child to distract Cástula, but at the end of the letter asked where Vicente was living, whom he was living with, and what he was doing. And she asked all this as if nothing had ever happened, as if that night, when she knew that Cástula wasn't going to have the longed-for baby, she hadn't abandoned her to her sorrow and her fate.

Cástula took her time in replying because she knew Sara would be on tenterhooks. She'd already waited a long time and could go on waiting.

Cástula's son had been born, that was true. From morning to night, she delighted in imagining Sara's face when she heard of the child's existence, when she saw his face and discovered the features of a beloved person, someone now far away, the only memory of whom left to her was those two black eyes.

The ghost of Vicente, like the memory of a dead person, was a clear and good idea, it was the dividing wall that would have finished off the house and covered the hole through which everything had escaped during those years, thought Sara. She'd been waiting so long for him that she'd forgotten to lay the foundations. And now, Cástula was sure, when the dividing wall of Vicente arrived, the house wouldn't be able to bear the load and would collapse.

Nights are cold in the desert, water freezes in basins. Cástula's black complexion was a weathered but soft skin and covered the warm organs it enclosed well. Pressing her belly, she curled up at the foot of a hill and fell asleep. A hand woke her at the moment when the cold was about to kill her.

What are you doing sleeping out here? asked the trader.

He was passing through on his wagon, breaking in a new white mule. He tried to raise Cástula, but she was stiff with cold, so he lit a fire beside her. When she woke, he said: Little mother, just look at where you've laid yourself down; this is no place for a pregnant woman. Then he held out a piece of dried meat to her. The taste is better when it's cooked in the smoke, he said, withdrawing another piece from the flames for himself. Let me tell you, mother, I sometimes think the soul is like a ghost trapped inside this machine. The trader pinched the skin of his arm and stretched it out. This machine, he said, a very complex machine, isn't it? Shall I tell you a story, lady? The story of a woman who, in the absence of her husband, became him. You'll say no, that's impossible. Yet that's how it was; she missed her husband so badly, she became him. People have seen her dressed like a rancher, with the hat and all, kissing the breasts of girls, and it seems like they are suckling each other . . .

Cástula hardly heard a word; although she was still numb with cold, her legs were loosening up and her whole body hurt as if someone had beaten her. Hasn't Sara come back? she asked. The trader was silent for a long time. Then he went on: The lady's husband only touched her once, on their wedding night, so she'd conceive. That may be why she clung to him— the things men do—but he never came back to her. When he left, she started to impersonate him, she walked like a man, dressed like a man, and she seduced girls like a man, it's said she sometimes even beat herself. The trader gave a cackle as he said this, with one hand on his belly and the other offering Cástula a second piece of meat. Meat cooked in the sun tastes better than raw meat. Aren't I right, lady? It doesn't even taste of mule now, it's like a fine steak.

How the trader laughed! Tears rolled down his cheeks. Cástula was sitting by the fire; it was just the smoke that made her eyes water. She looked down and her huge teardrops turned to dust as they fell into the ashes.

What name are you going to give the boy? asked the trader when he'd stopped laughing.

I don't know if it's a girl or a boy yet, said Cástula.

It should be born both, aren't I right, mother? That way you wouldn't have to choose. It seemed like his laughter was about to bubble over again, but Cástula interrupted to say: Juan, sir. I'm going to call him Juan.

That's a good name, lady; quite a common one, but strong, aren't I right? Soldier of God, I think it means, but don't take my word for it, I don't know much about such things. I knew a Juan a long while ago, one of those people who believe that God isn't present in this world and so spend their whole lives waiting for him to come. He was the type of man they call "a good soul" when he's dead, but alive everyone calls crazy. Juan was waiting for the coming of God, but the women arrived first, you know how it is. One in particular loved him. I've rarely seen such unconditional, absolute love. He was an ugly old man, all hunched over, and she was the prettiest girl in the town and very young, men paid a lot of money to watch her dance. She'd go to the river to wash afterwards because she thought being seen by men made her dirty, but that was how she made a living for herself, her sisters, and brothers. And Juan was always there, in the river. He believed that the voice of God could only be heard under the water and spent the whole day taking dips, and that's why everybody said Juan was crazy, spending all his time under the water in the river, talking to whoever cared to listen. And she always listened. She adored him, called him Maestro, and wherever she went she told people that Juan wasn't mad, that he was a wise man. Well, a whore will believe anything, they answered. And there you have it! All that devotion didn't work out for either of them, because, you see, the girl went to the river one day, resolved to tell Juan she loved him. He was there, as always, his body wrinkled with age and from so much time immersed in water. He was ugly as sin; when he was swimming, his body became paler, and when he stretched out he looked like a cat fetus, all red from the sun. What little hair he had was slicked behind his ears and his balding scalp shone in the sun, which was like a gold coin at that time. Juan, the girl said, I love you. I'm beautiful and I can have your child and teach it what you've taught me, and that child will do good because it will know about God from the moment it arrives. And guess what Juan said. He was unmoved by the sight of her, standing up to her knees in the water next to him, trying to take his hands. Cold as ice, he said: See here, child, I'm not interested in your body, or your face, or your hair. Get out of here and don't come bothering me again. I'm busy. And, lady, she left, and was so miserable and angry that she asked one of her lovers to kill Juan, to cut off his head so his blood would flow into the river and she would finally feel a little of the warmth of his body. Cástula was still crying; the smoke was by then blowing in another direction and not straight into her face, but she went on crying. The trader took her hands: Juan is a good name, lady, don't be frightened, I only wanted to tell you a story. She didn't hear him because her own voice drowned out the trader's. I'm going to call him Juan, she said, hugging her belly, I'm going to call him Juan. Yes, lady, it's a good name. Call him whatever you like, but stop crying.

Cástula had succeeded in finding Vicente. The trader had given her a gold coin and she'd used it to pay for transportation, food, and the beautiful yellow dress that hugged her lovely black body and made her visible at night. For the child's good luck, the trader had said. A coin, a small welcoming gift for your Juan. Cástula had more than thanked him that morning in the back of the wagon. Before setting her down, he said: If you're searching for a man, you'll know where to find him; look in the cantinas.

For weeks, Cástula went on wearing her same baggy, pink dress and talking to her belly. She slept curled up on sidewalks or stretched out on the pews of the church. She kept the gold coin close to her left breast in her grubby, threadbare brassiere, thinking to save it until her son was born.

The nuns gave her a blanket, but it was an elderly woman who took her in and fed her.

Jesusa was a learned and devout townswoman who earned her daily crust by her beautiful handwriting. She was the local scribe. When some storekeeper came to ask her to write to a debtor, he'd dictate vulgar threats and she'd write such an elegant, carefully worded letter that the debtor would pay up, although not always immediately. Jesusa was renowned for being able to achieve anything with a letter. She lived alone and in the town it was said that she'd aged so respectably because she'd never been in love.

One day, old Jesusa took Cástula by the hand and led her to her home. Cástula noted that her palms were very smooth, like those of the only children of rich parents who have never had to wash a pot. Jesusa put her in the bath, added hot water and freshly cut leaves from the lemon tree in the yard, and Cástula's rounded belly emerged from the infusion like a turtle. Where's the father? Jesusa asked. I'm searching for him, answered Cástula.

And what's this irresponsible man's name, my girl? I know people; together we might be able to find him.

His name is Vicente. Vicente Barrera.

Jesusa used her long fingers to braid Cástula's hair, as if the least tug would cause her mortal pain. While they were drinking fresh milk, she took her into the garden, taught her the names of some of the plants, and said: When the child starts to grow and begins to play, he'll want to nibble the flowers, but don't let him, Cástula, because there are flowers that have all too heavy souls. That purple one over there in the corner is used by women to tame men, but they say a girl who lives just around the corner here was given it in a soda on the day they were celebrating her engagement. That night she was seen walking all alone, naked. She said she was desperately searching for a man on horseback. The future husband saw her, we all saw her, she seemed to be caressing herself, she was all of a flutter, as they say of the hens. She'd anticipated her wedding night. Her mother ran out of the house with a blanket to try to fetch her back, with the whole town watching, but she couldn't catch up.

The next day, the girl returned, asleep on the back of a white mule, still naked. No one knows where she got the mule and she said she couldn't remember anything. Her fiancé had her examined and as she wasn't a virgin any longer, the engagement had to be broken off. The girl was so filled with sorrow that she threw herself from the bell tower of the church and though she wasn't killed, she was left half-witted.

That other flower, in the opposite corner, the fleshy one hanging like a bell: it might smell delicious, Cástula, but don't even think of making tea with it. And that tree at the end of the garden, well my girl . . . you have to be prepared for every eventuality. If your child isn't born alive or he goes and dies, take a few shoots and put them in his grave so he'll be born into eternal life.

Three weeks had gone by without Cástula's belly swelling any further, she listened carefully to the woman during their daily walks around the garden, but her mind was always on something else: Was the child dead? If Jesusa finds out, she won't want me here. Why would a decent lady take in a black woman like me, unless that woman were pregnant?

The milk had begun to drain from her breasts and only a sweet water oozed from her nipples, she didn't even feel that her hips were pulling apart as if they might snap in two.

Jesusa had discovered that Vicente was living just three hours from the town, in Boca de Perro, and that he was still selling yarns.

You have to demand your rights, child, but if you stay with me, I'll give you half of all I have; you don't need any help here, the tomatoes grow themselves and the avocado tree will start to bear fruit this year. Over there are the chickens, the bean plants flower all year round, we have water, Cástula, and if you stay, I'll teach your son to read.

Her old woman's eyes were always moist, but as she said this Jesusa trembled like the bags of water hung to scare away flies. Cástula said nothing, but she put an arm around the woman, stroked her hair, and they stayed like that for a while, one leaning on the other, until the younger of the two said good-night and left the older to her light sleep.

Early the next morning, drowsing in bed, Cástula watched in horror as her belly deflated like a balloon. Very soon her skin was sagging as if the child had already been born, but when she searched in and under the bed, there was nothing there. She hadn't even felt any pain, just the sensation that her liver, her lungs, and her guts were returning to their proper place. This can't be true, she told herself. Jesusa will throw me out. She checked her left breast, saw the gold coin beneath her tattered brassiere and, swaddled in the older lady's shawl, ran out of the house.

She cashed in the coin, bought a ticket, and stood waiting for the train in her new yellow dress, clutching a handful of the small purple flowers the lady had told her not to touch. The dress fitted snugly over her hips, and she noticed that her ass was drawing the eyes of men. She'd been wearing the pink shift for so long, it had never occurred to Cástula that anyone would find her desirable. Except for that woman or man, that night, in the house where things shone like they were permanently new.

This small pearl, hidden deep in this black rose; I'm going to lick it, she remembered the woman had said. And then the memory of her tongue and that pain, or something similar, a place in her own body that somebody else had discovered, closed her eyes.

Boca de Perro was a dusty place. It was late when she arrived and only the cantina was still open. You'll be better with beer than the water in that damned town, a man on the train had said, anyone who drinks the water never leaves. Cástula hadn't really been listening, the man had come up and started talking to her when she was absorbed in her own thoughts and, although the train was travelling slowly and steadily over the rails, he pretended to fall, rubbing the bulge in his pants like crazy. During those long moments of confusion, while she was attempting to push him off, the other passengers looked on and laughed. Damn darky, you think you're someone, don't you? he said when Cástula had managed to slip from his clutches, and then he spat a green gob onto her shoes.

Her black shoes, the first new shoes she'd had in her whole life, with comfortable heels that weren't worn down, and lined with pigskin rather than rubber, her beautiful shoes covered in the green phlegm of that son of a bitch, that animal, that fucking pig. Cástula had swallowed the insults welling up in her gullet, understanding that, as a woman of color, she'd be despised in that place. If she'd spoken out while on the train, everyone would have laughed, they'd have been capable of lining up to spit in her face. And when she got off the train and was walking along, dying of thirst and looking for water, some children shouted: Fucking shit brown darky.

It made no difference that she had bills stuffed in her brassiere and a fine new dress, she was still a "fucking darky." That was why she felt at ease in the cantina and, anyway, she desperately needed something to drink. Rage had dried her throat; everything she hadn't said for months was bursting to get out. The heat of her silence was an inferno, but the beer cooled it. No one bothered her there, at that hour the drunks were slouched across the tables like corpses. The owner of the place said: Welcome, what can I get you? And she replied, Something to drink, please. The man laughed and then opened two beers, saying: On the house.

Her first night in Boca de Perro was sleepless. Drinking alongside men like sacks of guts made her feel powerful, the alcohol poured straight into her bloodstream, cleansing her, or that's what it felt like: the cleansing of an ancestral resentment.

Need to find a hotel, she said as she rose unsteadily when day was beginning to break, and the cantinero replied: Why do you want a hotel when you've got my bed in here, momma.

They slept together, but he was incapable of doing anything. He fell asleep with his hand on his genitals and for some time she observed his body, sprawled across the mattress. She didn't feel the least tenderness or desire for him. Both he and his dark, miserable hovel reeked of piss, and every corner of the tiny bedroom was littered with bottles and trash, the nauseating poverty of the drunkard.

When he woke, she said: Have a beer with me, baby, just look at the face on you. She seemed desperate to start the day with a drink. That's my girl, he said, giving her a slap on the ass. Cástula had thrown away the remains of the purple flowers after boiling them for hours to extract every ounce of their strength; she'd left the liquid to cool and then poured it into the cantinero's alcohol. It was a matter of simple curiosity, with no particular end in view; although she didn't know why, she wanted this man's devotion. While she was doing all that, she remembered Jesusa telling her the story of the girl who had returned naked on a white mule, but she tried to keep her thoughts on other things. There was something mechanical about it all, her body, the rhythm with which her thoughts came and went, everything moved inside her as if she had a chronometer there that had been designed at the very beginning of time by some hand that wasn't hers.

The man slept through the whole morning and she opened the bar. When she spotted that a client was drunk, she'd ask if he knew a certain Vicente Barrera. Sometimes they'd say: That's me, momma, what can I do for you? or Vicente's dead, or That doggone son of a bitch fucks anything that moves, or Here I am, negrita, come and get it.

In the late afternoon, the cantinero appeared. He behaved like a tame puppy with her. What a quality woman does, he told Cástula, grabbing her breast and putting his other hand into her panties, what a quality woman does is send her man straight to sleep after a night of hot sex. She felt like spitting in his face, but gently pushed him away, saying: I'll leave you to take care of the store, I've got things to do. The cantinero watched her depart through the door and immediately burst into tears, as if she'd died. You look fucking awful, said a man who had recently come in and was drinking in a dark corner.

Go to hell, Vicente. What would you know about love? the cantinero sobbed.

They said you were looking for me and here I am. How can I help you?

So this is the man Sara's so madly in love with, thought Cástula, not the least understanding how a beast that drooled all over the girls when he was dancing could keep anyone waiting with bated breath. But when Vicente moved close, his voice was so warm it filled Cástula's ears. And when he gazed at her with those enormous black eyes that gave her the exact same sense of desolation as looking out a door into absolute darkness, she wanted him. She felt a need to care for him, to rock him between her breasts and feed him a little of the sad water that trickled from them in place of milk.

I've travelled a long way to sleep with you, she breathed in his ear. Vicente gave a laugh. Just sleep with me, negrita? And Cástula held his gaze.

There's nothing like that moment just before sex, not even the sex itself is better, nothing like the burning pulse of those moments when no one is quite ready to make the first move. Yet Vicente had said: Listen, leave me alone, negrita. It'll be your fault if the cantinero won't serve me anymore. And he'd quickly turned away to sit with a young girl who was waiting for him, continuing to observe her with a mocking expression.

Cástula stood where she was for a few minutes, then picked up a rag to wipe the counter. In the pauses in her task, she raised a bottle of aguardiente to her lips.

What were you doing with Vicente, Cástula? Can't you see he's a married man? He comes here with his wife and a hooker starts flirting with him. Show a little respect, girl. The cantinero was jealous, you could see it a mile off. I know you don't love me, but I love you, negrita, and if you stay with me, I can give you a good life, I'll even cut down on the drink. You come to live with me, you help me keep the place clean and serve that vermin, and then we'll go far away, to the beach if you like, and I'll be sure you have those delicious salted chocho dumplings, every day if that's what you want, negrita. What about it? He'd grabbed her waist and was rubbing himself up against her, with his disgusting breath in her face. The man smells just like rotting meat, thought Cástula, reminded of a dead dog with flies buzzing around it. And unable to bear any more, she pushed him away, saying: Get off me, you pig. And just for that he yelled, waved his hands about, and slapped her face several times. All she could do in return was spit at him until her saliva dried up and, mixing with the blood, covered her face too. Nobody tried to get between them, not even Vicente, who looked on impassively, covering the eyes of the child who accompanied him.

I see the fool's gone and fallen in love, Castulita, said Vicente the next day when he came across her in the street. Lucky you. Why do you think that man's single when he has the only business in this damn town making any money?

Cástula was not at all sure if he meant the owner of the cantina had killed his other women or that they had left him. She sat under a tree, holding a slice of aloe vera to her swollen lip and burst into tears. Vicente came to sit beside her and said: Come on, girl, I'll give you a hug, stop crying.

Is that child who was with you in the cantina yesterday your wife? she asked, and Vicente replied by putting a hand on her leg, kneading and pinching the inside of her thigh as he moved it upward. What's it to you, darky? A man's a man, he said. And just what does that mean? replied Cástula. Vicente looked carefully up and down the street and, with a hand on her shoulder, guided her to a nook between two large rocks. He lowered her panties and, without so much as a kiss, moved two fingers inside her.

Let's see if that's enough for you, negrita, he said and left.

Cástula pulled up her panties and stood there, alone, with the whole weight of her body on her bent knees, as she waited for the wave of heat to pass and was capable of walking back to the street.

An instinct for expecting the worst had warned Cástula what a mistake it might be to fall in love with him. All men have something horrible hidden inside them. There was no doubting that. But, even so, Cástula felt nothing, was by then incapable of feeling. She was a black, shapeless mass, making her way aimlessly through the world like a dried up glasswort. When she suddenly found herself able to reflect on her surroundings, she wondered why there were so few women in the town. The ones she'd seen were others like herself, worn out, scarred, letting the men put it in and out without so much as a flicker of expression on their faces to show the difference between pleasure and distaste. The only woman who stood out, reminding her of something she'd lost long ago, before the first kidnapping, the first child, before Jesusa and that bitch Sara, was Vicente's wife. But naturally, she would stand apart; the child was scarcely twelve years old. She was too young to know anything. If only. And judging by the way her husband treated her, she was still unspoiled goods. Her legs were straight, without that bow you get from having it rammed in. That damn child even smells of poop, of diapers and piss. Cástula felt like her head was ready to explode with rage just thinking of it. She hated her, hated the way all the men treated her with such delicacy, as if she was a newborn babe that might break at any moment.

And is that child you brought in here supposed to be your daughter, your whore, or your servant, Vicente? she asked the following day and everybody in the cantina stared. You're getting into hot water there, negrita, muttered a drunk. Don't you dare even mention that girl to me, you miserable darky. I love her more than my fucking mother, snapped Vicente, dragging her by the braids. He threw her into a corner behind the bar among the trash, pulled down his pants, lifted her skirt, and after using Cástula's hand to work his dick, began the frenzied in-out ritual of humping her. She looked into space, her hair sticking to the sweat on her forehead. How lovely it had been to have no history when she'd lived in a small town, doing no harm to anyone; how lovely it had been to breastfeed the baby when it was alive and for the milk to flow even if she hadn't eaten. That had been sheer magic. The child's laughter as it slept, and then, later, Lazarito's as he ran through the streets, covered in dust. You look like a ghost, Lazarito. Go take a bath, you savage.

And now, finally, if things worked out, Lázaro would have a brother with the same blood, a gift for him and a slap in the face for Sara. Cástula had believed it was worth putting up with the stink of that man and the humiliation, the huge humiliation of all those days, and of being fucked in the piss of drunks.

A few months later, when it seemed the whole business had been forgotten, she persuaded the cantinero to kill Vicente. Her exact words were: Look, all you have to do is bury this in the back of his head and that rat will be dead in no time at all. He agreed, said he loved her, would do anything for his negrita, that together they would this and together that, and far, far away. Cástula had already taken control of his money. I'll administer this, my love, and just wait and see how I'll make it grow. They had walked to Vicente Barrera's home, armed with a machete, but as they passed through the gate, they saw the girl sitting under an orange tree and the cantinero confessed: I'm frightened, Cástula. I've never killed a man before.

The girl was dressed in white with her long, black hair falling below her waist. That child looks like death; I can't do it, I'm too scared. Don't worry, she replied, You're not going to kill anyone. Your task is going to be easier; go get her, I've got another idea.

The girl was asleep, her half-open, wide eyes allowed a glimpse of the whites, like slivers of moon. They were both high on hard liquor when they went for her. Lie her down on the ground, I want to see how you fuck her, and if you won't, I'll never do it with you again, and you'll just have to go on hoping, Cástula told him.

Whenever he wanted to sleep with her, she'd get the cantinero drunk or find other ways to distract him. She'd work things so he was always left wanting her more than the day before, more deeply in her service.

Lying on top of the girl with her panties already in his hand, the cantinero said: I can't, Cástula, I just can't. This child hasn't even grown breasts yet. It's you I want to be with, I don't like this. Let's get out of here.

It was clear the girl was used to those shenanigans, clear that Vicente had tried to do the same more than once, but, like them, had more than once been stopped by the child's eerie serenity.

You're not man enough for it, you're just a no-good coward and you've failed me. Cástula slapped the cantinero again and again and in this way they departed the scene, banging the metal gate behind them, leaving the girl lying on the ground, her arms wide open, like a Christ figure.

Jesusa had told her that, up to a few years back, there were only two people left in her bloodline: herself and her sister, two rich, good-looking heiresses who were very much alone in the world. My sister was so lovely, Cástula, you can't imagine how lovely, she was the most beautiful woman I've ever seen, and I say *was* because Lupita, God rest her soul, died one day while I was arranging her hair. Right here in my arms, she went and died as if she'd been dealt a fatal blow to the head; I've never been so terrified in all my life. I was braiding her beautiful black hair when the blood started to seep into it and I said: Sis, what's going on? But she couldn't hear me by then. The police had to come. Everyone had to come. The house was full of gawkers, and they were all staring at me as if I were capable of . . . Jesusa choked up, Cástula had to fetch a glass of water so she could continue her story. She listened as carefully as children do when they hide under the table to hear the grown-ups' secrets, holding their breath so nobody knows they are there.

I did my very best to find out what had happened to Lupita, to save my reputation; reputation is everything in these small towns. You know that, don't you Cástula? That's why you've been looking for the father of your child and that's why I visited the witch. The town forgave me when they got her answer. That horrible woman told me someone had been jealous of Lupita's wealth and beauty, and that person had buried a pair of her drawers in the cemetery so she'd never be happy or would die. My poor Lupita, so handsome, so good, said old Jesusa, resting her head in Cástula's roughened hands.

These hands, noted Cástula as she lay awake in the darkness and the dogs barked, the same hands that stole the panties of Vicente's girl to make her die. After they had fled, she'd left the cantinero sleeping in the shack and there, in the cemetery, the animals watched her dig a hole and drop the child's white panties into it. That same day, she left and went back to being the wandering negrita, going from town to town, living through whole stretches of months that never added up to years. When she left, she took the wad of bills she'd stolen from the cantinero. The money was for her child, Lazarito's brother, who was already causing her breasts and belly to swell once again.

I'll name him Juan, she thought. I'm going to name him Juan and he's going to be a strong boy, a good boy, nobody will love him more than I do and that means he'll be the man who defends me from men.

When the child was born, Cástula didn't feel the way she'd expected. Even while he was a part of her, maternal feelings had started to lose their edge, it wasn't like the first time: the immense companionship of someone she didn't yet know and then the overwhelming impact of seeing her newborn son, still covered in blood, latching to her breast to feed. It wasn't the same. When Juan cried, the sound was unbearable, his expression as he fed from her breasts scared her. He was like a small, wrinkled old man, a baby that inspired sheer fright. Deep down, Cástula sensed that the problem wasn't the child, it was because she was a broken woman. At some point she'd lost the ability to be the person she once was: she didn't recognize her present self in the young girl who used to watch the boys running around, itching to join them, to make them laugh at her playacting; she wasn't the negrita who did favors for everyone, who never allowed herself to be offended by anything when she could display her row of gleaming white teeth like a gesture of truce with the world. Now everything brought disdain and indifference in its wake. And if she'd attempted to kill someone, well, she hadn't carried it through. She went from cantina to cantina, challenging the drunks: No one here can look me in the eyes and say he's never wanted to kill someone, no one in this crap joint has the balls to tell me what he's done! Because I have. I killed a child who looked like death! Give it a rest, woman, the drunks said, all you did was bury a child's panties and now it turns out you've got superpowers. Come on over here and I'll show you how I can bury something else in you. Noise, pure and simple, that's what those men's voices were. Cástula found it impossible to understand what they were saying, everything she saw was a blur and most of the things that happened in her life passed unnoticed in a haze of alcohol, as if she were moving underwater or as slowly as a slug in a drought.

Juan took his first steps tugging on the cord that tied him to the bed while he waited for her to come home. At first he used to cry, later he resigned himself to believing that was how the world was, the natural succession of the events of his life.

One night, when Cástula returned, she forced him to drink alcohol. Juan fell into a deep sleep and, unsteady though she was, Cástula managed to lay him in a large egg box, put the box on a handcart, and, struggling with her heavy load, walk to the doors of the bus station.

Once a week, a bus ran to the largest town in the area, rounding curves and dodging landslips. Cástula didn't even know if she'd been planning this for some time or if the drink had helped her to decide that the moment had come. She paid the driver double fare to take the package to Jesusa's house and he agreed, thinking it was money for old rope. Take good care of my box, there's something fragile in there. Let me put it here, right beside you as if it were a passenger.

Old Jesusa will love him, she needs him, Cástula thought as she returned to the bar; the boy will have a good life, he'll be brought up by a good person and not an ungrateful black woman who didn't know how to love the son she'd prayed for so hard.

Like all drunks, Cástula had lost any sense of time. It didn't enter her head that Jesusa might by then be dead and so, however much she wanted, unable to open the door. It didn't enter her head that, on throwing down the package and so accidentally opening it, the frightened driver would find Juan pale and vomiting and, thinking he was at death's door, would leave him outside the hospital, where he would be rehydrated through the large vein that runs over the scaphoid bone of the foot, at the risk of being left lame, and that he would eventually—as the strongest puppies do—survive, despite having worms. Or that the crippled Juan would grow to manhood between an orphanage and the militia.

He'd taken the decision because at the end of each semester, when everyone said goodbye and went home to their families, he was left alone like a dog among the flea-infested bunks. The smell of damp wood, feet, and the sorrow of not loving anybody. Until one day, that strange band of soldiers arrived at the orphanage to say the army was like a family. During their whole speech, Juan had been thinking that his father was like them or was maybe even one of them. Join up. Your country needs you, boys, they'd said, and he'd stepped forward, with all the doubts of someone signing a blood pact. And that was why, for most of his life, he knew nothing but war.

And that was why, for Juan, Lázaro was a novelty, something better than he ever thought he'd deserve. Deep within himself, he was always aware of such a sharp sense of dejection that it was often transformed into the clear image of a well of dark water. It was a fantasy or a dream: he'd approach the well, climb up, supporting himself on the pulley, look down, and the liquid would invite him in. He'd spend hours, crouching, remembering, looking into the well, until he'd raise his head when Lázaro, standing above him, would catch his eye. There was no need to say anything, they'd just look at each other and after a few moments the well would open up inside Lázaro too. Ah, but he was able to move away, turn his back, walk off, trying to forget what he'd seen until the memory faded. Then he'd come back with that ingenuous smile and say: Juan, tell me something; Juan, come here, I'd like to leave this place. Juan would feel the urge to punch him. He wanted to make him suffer so he'd understand where that bad dream came from; so that, with them both finally knowing and understanding the same thing, they'd be closer to being a single person.

Juan hated speaking, he hated having to say the words "I feel."

Leave me in peace, you no-good whore, he'd yell, and go to squat before the fire.

Juan, the boy soldier who had been left outside a hospital and spent his childhood in an orphanage, had grown up with a body scarred by the caresses of priests, until one day the army offered him true salvation. So much pain had been stored in his well that it was now almost full.

There was no salvation, but at times the nearest thing to it was being close to Lázaro's body. And so much guilt, so much horror and fear loomed over Juan when he became aware of this.

If my father had lived, things would have been different. Growing up with a man would have made me one. If I'd had a father, I wouldn't have to love Lázaro, I'd love a woman, the normal way, the way God decrees. I'm telling you, Lázaro, if I'd been brought up by a man, I wouldn't love you, I don't love you, I think you're contemptible, you revolt me, but we have no other choice. Fucking girlyboy, fucking bitch, go wiggle your hips somewhere else.

Lázaro would watch him from the other side of the cave as the fire grew stronger, projecting its tenuous shadows onto the wall and casting its light on the sleeping bats. I haven't done you any harm, Juan, he'd say. And then he'd be silent, as he so often was, observing a clod of earth or trying to crumble a piece of rock between two fingers.

But when Lázaro died, all Juan's pain was returned to him. That's exactly how it was. He felt as if a pendulum had swung back and carried him so far from himself that he would never find that brokenhearted self again. And after watching Lázaro die, to find then that photo at the bottom of the sack and recognize his own father, the moron of a father he'd only seen twice in his life.

The first was the day he came to the house drunk to beat up Cástula, who'd also had too much to drink. Juan saw how he'd taken her by the hair and accused her of things, and then, when he was done beating her and she was lying unconscious on the floor, he looked Juan in the eyes and spat on the ground, shouting: Don't get it into your head that I'm ever going to recognize you as my son.

That's how he knew the man was his father.

The second was also the last time he saw Cástula. Vicente had barged into the house, saying: If that girl dies, I'll kill you, you damned souse.

A few weeks before, she'd sent his father a letter saying: *It might not have happened yet, but your girl is going to die one day, when you least expect it, and she'll die because I'll have killed her.* She wanted him to come and find her and she remembered that there was a direct link between his rage and his libido, but when he arrived she'd snidely told him about the panties, and the argument got so heated that he'd ended by believing he had to torture her to make her confess where they were, but she was so drunk, so lost to time and space, that she passed out after the fifth blow.

Later, Cástula woke in a memory.

At the moment she came round after the beating, she thought she was searching for her first child, dragging her badly bruised body along the floor of the shack only to find him lying cold and blue. Again, once again, she was going to pick up the dead baby and sit staring at him in horror for hours, unable to keen for him. On that occasion, she'd been so badly injured, so violated, so broken—just like on the night when Vicente returned—that her grief felt like the whole world's grief. So, still dazed from the beating, she allowed herself to fall into that flashback, to feed Juan alcohol, put him in a box, and send him far away.

That was his father. That was his mother. That was Juan, who, once he'd put the pieces of the puzzle together, came up with the plan of seeking out Vicente and killing him, finally getting his revenge on him for leaving, for having fucked his mother and Lázaro's mother, and who knows how many other women, sowing the seed of his cursed bloodline everywhere he passed.

Carrying the letters on his back as if they were rocks, Juan arrived in the appointed place. Cástula, his mother, the immaculate young girl, had done a good job.

Juan found Vicente's house.

III
The Anagrammatic Body

Before going into the supermarket to make the necessary purchases, María said goodbye as if she were never coming back; then she kissed his forehead and got out of the car. You're crazy, he said, although she was by then out of earshot; she passed the guard and the glass door opened as she approached.

In the heat the strip of concrete was emitting diaphanous flames, the ground was buckling and Salvador fell asleep watching it.

It was five in the afternoon when he woke. The heat had died down a little but María hadn't returned. Maybe she'd gotten bored watching him sleep or had felt hungry.

Salvador got out of the car and walked to a yellow stall gleaming in the distance. She wasn't there. And she wasn't at the flower stall either; there was no trace of her in the whole complex of awnings and guy ropes. A strong smell of rotting fruit hung in the air. Salvador went on searching, walking through all the places María might possibly be, and when he didn't find her, he decided to enter the supermarket.

Anxiety was beginning to churn his guts. He experienced something like nausea every time the thought that she'd decided to leave him entered his head. Why hadn't she told him? After so many years together, how could she have chosen to end it all in this way?

Before passing through the glass door, as if knowing that once inside all his fears would become realities, he made up his mind to keep cool and talk to the guard.

It was the same man as three hours before, standing stoically impassive. Salvador said: I'm looking for a woman. Good afternoon, answered the guard. I'm looking for a woman, Salvador repeated. What does the woman look like? responded the guard's expressionless face. A woman, Salvador repeated once again. And then he realized that the descent into a panic loop was affecting his speech: he was using the same letters to form the same two words. He felt as though he'd forgotten his own language and "a woman" was the only thing he truly understood. He clung to those two words and continued to utter them without pause before everything he knew could disappear. What does the woman look like, what does the woman look like, what does the woman look like? the guard responded, holding his gun a little tighter each time.

He couldn't remember María's body. He couldn't even remember if María was a man or a woman, because he couldn't even remember the name of the person he was missing so much.

I think it was a woman, Salvador eventually said, recovering a little confidence. The guard loosened his grip. If you don't tell me what this woman looks like, I can't help you.

Salvador couldn't remember María. He didn't remember her body, her face, or her hair. He did remember something about long, flowing tresses, but the image was mixed with the waves of heat rising from the sidewalk in the midday sun.

Sir, listen to me. You have to tell me the name of the person you're looking for and what she looks like, otherwise I can't help you.

The guard took his role very seriously. His eyes expressed nothing besides the automatic habit of obedience. Salvador was struggling with the bodies and faces walled up in his memory. Who were all those people presenting themselves in line before the one he was looking for? He looked down, clasping his hands, his face red with rage. Finally, he recalled a pair of eyes, or better, the sensation of looking into them. How could he explain that to the guard? He stammered something and while the man in the uniform went on asking him questions that seemed to have no answer, tears of frustration started to roll down his cheeks.

Sir, if you don't tell me what the woman looks like, I can't help you, shouted the man as Salvador slowly doubled over.

I can't remember, sir. I can't remember.

MARÍA

Perhaps the greatest test of human will is making up your mind. It wasn't dragging your body to work each day or forcing yourself to give up certain types of food. The greatest test of the will is deciding, despite all, to continue existing. That's more difficult than deciding to end someone else's life, because when you die, anything that could produce a change in the world in which one's own will functions dies too.

Salvador has never understood why his mother was killed. There's no motive, he said, but if I hadn't been so afraid of being alone after my father died, I wouldn't have met you. He asserted this with conviction, but I can't really remember how we found each other. He always said it was while he was running away from his hometown because he thought he was being stalked by the same man who killed his mother. That's all he says on the subject. The only thing I'm certain of is that it was scorching hot that summer and I spent a lot of time cooling my feet in the river. The water smelled swampy and green scum would lap between my toes, but that was the best I could do: a creek hidden among a complex of tall glass buildings and miserable shacks covered in the dust the strong desert winds blow in. I remember I found him sleeping there. I watched him until he opened his eyes, and then we talked the whole afternoon, not holding anything back, like children, or old people who have spent their whole lives together.

Another of the tests of human will is deciding to love the same person forever. It's almost like the decision to continue to exist, so that life will be the same for as long as our bodies survive. It's deciding to share that body with one person, and although others might enter, the decision implies not allowing them to open the doors leading to places from which you can never eject them. That's why I didn't understand when I saw another shadow inside Salvador. After seeing him with that woman, my whole day was plagued by a sense of foreboding. For instance, I dreamed the world was tumbling down and as it fell, we found it was made of some light material, incapable of harming us. I was upset because when I saw everything collapsing, I felt a sort of relief, thinking that by the end of the dream I too would be destroyed. Yet when I opened my eyes, I was still alive in a crumbling world.

Why do you do these things to me, Salvador? I asked when I woke. He stared at me. I think I love her, he said.

There was a time when everything was fine. Or that's what I thought.

Like that day; while we were hiking, a pair of birds passed us, and then the birds fell to the ground.

Did you see that? I asked, but Salvador didn't stop to look, he went on walking, listening to his own voice—always weak when he sang—issue from his mouth.

It's dangerous to hike where nobody else does, he suddenly pronounced, almost in a shout.

He was annoyed, truly annoyed with me, because on that trip we'd decided to hike off the beaten track. When I suggested that we'd be okay, we were together and had a knife, he snapped: How can you be sure that I really am here?

Maybe he was already tired of me, because, after a while without saying another word, he ran off into the llano, so far that I lost sight of him in the blue hues of the distant hills.

We were hungry but hadn't wanted to kill rabbits. Salvador always became grouchy when he hadn't eaten. I knew he'd be back, so I sat down and waited there for him.

I passed the time thinking of the day my mother abandoned me outside the supermarket. That memory—which rarely came into my mind, and on this occasion was sparked by something as simple as Salvador running off—took up residence and discreetly grew into a sensation, a virus.

My mother abandoned me, although, to be honest, she did later come back. She was crying when she returned. Her eyes were red and brimming with tears, we boarded a bus and never again mentioned the subject, or at least not until I was an adult and asked her what had happened. She told me I'd imagined the whole thing: You just imagined it all, María, how silly of you to think that; you must have wandered off in the supermarket or I went to put something in the trolley. Wow, the way children exaggerate things!

I was only four, but I can't have gotten it wrong: she'd put some bills in my pocket and a piece of paper with writing on it that I kept until it vanished from the notebook where I'd stashed it. She took it from me before I could learn to read.

I remember I made a huge effort to try to read and write my name because of that note, as though that simple achievement would immediately endow me with what I considered adult superpowers.

I used to crawl under the table with a marker pen and, hidden there, write in red letters: A I R A M.

When he returned, Salvador was carrying a hare. I had to kill it, he said. We roasted it over an open fire and I was frightened when the flames caused the body to make a noise like thunder. Later, when we were resting on our improvised seats of rock, we saw another animal skipping near a gulley and Salvador asked if I was still hungry.

It took me a moment to realize he was joking, because I was in fact still hungry. And as always, without me having to say a word, he knew. He stretched out his arm to offer me his last piece of hare.

Don't you get bored of always knowing what I'm thinking? I asked. Don't you get bored of always knowing when I'm lying and when I'm telling the truth? When I tell you the damn truth, Salvador. Do you really not get fed up?

Salvador didn't bat an eye. It was infuriating to see him so unmoved. He laughed.

I shouted: I wish you were dead! And then I ran to find a place far from him, where the hills begin to turn blue. I ran so far that I discovered the hills aren't blue when you get there.

When I tired and was on my way back, I came across three leverets searching for their mother. I tried not to think about what we'd just eaten, about that fatty belly, those full hare breasts.

One day, I ran away from my mother. We were in the supermarket again and she let go of my hand because, when she leaned down to look at me, I spit in her face and said I hated her. Then I ran and hid behind a stand to cry. Even I didn't understand what I'd just done.

Buy me something, Mom, buy me something, Mom, buy me something, buy me something, I whined, walking behind her in the supermarket. Buy me something, Mom, buy me something. And she was uptight, I don't know why, maybe looking for something we couldn't find. I remember that she picked up small things and put them in her bag. She said: Shhh, María, don't say anything; I'm out of cash.

I always thought she was lying when she said she didn't have any money. I even thought she said it to annoy me, thought my mother had a prettier house than ours and that when she left me alone, tied by a cord to our bed, saying she was going to work, she was really going to her other house, where there were a lot of trees and lots of furniture, and there would be lots of cake too. I thought that when she put her card in the ATM, it handed out however much money she wanted, but her idea was to annoy me by not sharing the cake we savored from a distance in store windows.

My mother had a lovely pair of shoes with spangles, high heels, and diamonds on the ankle straps. And when I found the place where she hid the shoes, I told myself that my mother was rich and wore those shoes when she went all dressed up to her other life. I put them back and never asked about them. But that day in the supermarket, when I pleaded and pleaded for something and she gave me nothing, I remembered the shoes and turned red with rage. I could feel my face burning and the veins throbbing at my temples, but I waited patiently until she took me from the shopping trolley to run far away from her and her lies.

When she approached, I was scared. I crawled from stand to stand, until a woman took my hand and led me to the area where they made announcements about things and lost people.

I heard them announce the name I'd made up so my mother wouldn't come to fetch me, but she knew it was me, because the alias that sounded in the pauses in a tropical song was her name.

Salvador and I wanted to go to the forest, we thought it would be easy to get there without a map, but we were both lost. Then we stopped squabbling and decided to walk to a spot in the mountain we could see in the distance, where the endless grassland was less lush.

When we arrived, we came across a group of very short men. We didn't understand their language, but they gestured us to sit in a circle, held out some jars, and invited us to drink. We sang and danced until, without warning, a bolt of lightning hit one of the men.

Befuddled from what we'd drunk, I was daydreaming that I was on a journey to the interior of myself and, using a bone as a slide, I descended to an artery behind which an old lady was hidden. What are you looking at? she asked sharply and I replied: I want answers. Roaring with laughter, the old woman said: Come back when you've got a question. And she looked so funny that I had to laugh with her; her left leg was a cow's and her nipple was gilded. This woman is a scream, I thought, and my laughter gradually drew me out of my dream.

I found myself facing the man who had been struck by lightning. He wasn't dead. Salvador was playing at touching the other's face with his tongue, and said: María, magpie, come and look at this, he's electrified. He was a muscular man, with almost black skin and hair falling down below his ass.

I understood from one of the others that before he was born, the man had been lightning and that was why the bolt had respected his body and allowed him to go on living.

That night, while everyone was dancing in the darkness, the short, very dark man, with my full consent, skewered me with his long penis. I took it in my hands and found it was a stone battering ram, but when it entered me it became softer. He started to shudder slowly, until he got as far as he could possibly go, at which point my insides prevented the entry of his whole body, from head to toe. And then I realized I was on the verge of falling back. I felt like I was being thrown from the carousel on which I'd been securely mounted forever. I thought: My guts hadn't been able to prevent that small man from entering right into me. My whole body enfolded him and it seemed as though he were incarnate inside me, the way a collar that is being constantly tugged ends up digging into the neck of a chained dog. I saw Salvador in the background, fanning the flames and singing.

I felt a profound hatred of him.

The next day, on the improvised bed of embers covered by damp earth, it wasn't the short, black man who lay beside me, but Salvador.

He was still Salvador.

I had a father too. A sort of poor substitute for a father. His name was Jesús. He wasn't always with my mother and me. I remember that when I was young, I saw him launching himself at children, biting them. He once bit me and I thought I was going to die, choked by my own wails rather than from the pain. I've always believed those bruises were the same color as the skin of the first dead body I saw when I was working in the morgue; or that became my inevitable association; I had a panic attack on that occasion too.

My father disappeared after the bite attack and didn't return until I was a teenager. My mother thanked God for having brought him back: You really will have a father now, she told me, and she covered my face in kisses, leaving it smeared with lipstick I didn't know she possessed. Even though I'd almost completely forgotten my father, I was frightened of him; I think my body did remember. And it was right to do that: Jesús became the animal I knew best. I never had a pet; there was no need, I had my father. He wasn't a human being, my father was something different. A dog that wasn't quite a dog. A dog that had once been a man, and if a man were to be changed into a dog, you can imagine how strong the fury of his confusion would be. Jesús would run circles on the spot the way a hungry wolf does when it's trying to follow the fading scent of a trail of blood that is soaking into the ground somewhere in the desert.

I imagined that in his mind he was always hunting a corpse. A half-dead corpse isn't the same as the previous body, the live body; it's a different entity, merely something for the remaining animals to fight over: mammals, worms, cute puppies, and carrion birds all want their share.

In my mind, my father was always a solitary, hungry wolf, a feeble dog. I'd sometimes try to put myself in his place: I'd imagine the desperation of longing for his human body, and not being able to communicate it. When he tried to speak, the rest of us heard growls. For Jesús, it must have been like witnessing his own death from the outside. Sometimes, when he was looking at me, I'd notice that his dog's body felt desire for a female body, my body. The body of a dog longing for something unlike, something that wasn't—as he was—"a beast."

At times my mother, wearing that new lipstick she started to buy when he returned, would go off to a room with him and they'd both shout. Other than that, the poor dog, my father, was alone because there was no other animal like him. He was a one-dog pack. His family very soon turned their backs on him and sent him to live chained up in a darkened room. He became a living corpse; like a love affair gone bad: something that stank, but had to be kept until it rotted away. In part he was in that room because electric light had an adverse effect on him. Light cracked his skin, weathered it in an instant as if he'd spent days in the wind.

He was sent to live in darkness, where he ended by becoming the thing he'd be when he died. One evening, I was left alone with him again and when they came back, they found me with bites and gleaming purple marks on every inch of my body. I remember the color, only the color and the sensation of a scream that just wouldn't emerge. My mother said it was the second time she had to slap me to make me breathe.

Jesús had been locked up for years without anyone but us visiting him. No one cared about him. It was worse than if he'd died, because you miss dead people, cry for them, set them on a pedestal. But not Jesús; Jesús still had a body and that made a difference. The last person to visit him was a friend of mine who was curious about the rumors he'd heard going around the town and asked if we could see him together. We can go together, I said, but I'll wait outside. And that's what we did.

When he came out, the boy fainted in front of me as he was telling me about it: He's got hair, María, hair all over his body and he walks on all fours, and his eyes, his eyes . . .

When my friend came round, he was different too. I didn't realize it at first, because I loved him, because the love you feel at that age is the passionate kind: we alone choose the other because it feels good to have them close, because we desire them and our bodies are satisfied by theirs. Naturally, at times I'd think: This is it, this is as good as it gets. But you grow up, meet more people, and realize that you never really knew much about that person who could have been the father of your children if all those rubbers you used when you discovered sex hadn't worked.

My friend said that my father lunged at him, but the chain had stopped him just before the bars, his own impetus had dragged him back and he was coughing and choking; my friend said he was so frightened he began to scream and my father went back to sit in a far corner like a trembling animal and, from there, he raised his head and the two of them looked into each other's eyes for a long moment. And that's why what happened happened. Venom, my father had venom in his eyes.

The scene in this movie makes me really uncomfortable because it reminds me of Jesús. A man with Alzheimer's is sitting in the sun, reading. In the pauses he takes to fix his eyes on the newspaper or book that's been chosen for him, his daughter wipes away the spittle trickling from his mouth; the man has forgotten he needs to close it. The books and newspapers have been selected for the sole purpose of being placed in the man's hands; they date from the long past years when the daughter who wipes away the spittle used to run beside him while they played at getting to wherever it was first. The spittle has damaged much of the paper, the pages of the books are wrinkled, the glue of the binding has worn away, pages fall out and nobody picks them up. The man is holding the yellowing book upside down because he isn't reading it, the man is going through the motions of the act of reading. His memory is on the point of collapse, he'll soon forget to breathe and will suffocate, although possibly by that time he'll have forgotten that he's a man. He's very close to that state and yet still recalls the routine of sitting in the sun to read a book. He doesn't know what he's reading and that doesn't matter to him. I often wonder what's passing through that man's mind when he looks at the book as if he's reading. Why did he retain that impulse while so many others, like closing his mouth, were lost? Why does he remember that, but not his children's faces? He's always giving them clips around the ear, thinking they are intruders. Most of all I think: If the man no longer has any memory, what is going on in his head when he moves his eyes? If he isn't reading or remembering, what does he see? What are his eyes doing when they stare into space? Maybe seeing, simply seeing. But what can you see when memory has ceased to exist?

I've always thought that scene was about something you have inside you, something that can go on seeing, even after death.

I learned that too while I was working in the morgue; but I still don't know what allows us to see despite being dead.

The only conclusion we came to at the time was that it was witchcraft. A spell transmitted during the lengthy eye contact that occurred between my father and some man. I was immune, I'd go down to look in his eyes and say with mine: Hey, dog, here I am, come and get me. I did it to annoy him, so he'd hurt himself crashing into the bars of his cage, because I knew he couldn't stop himself pulling on his chain, torturing himself while I looked into his eyes, leaping at me even though it would choke him.

Very soon afterwards my friend also started walking on all fours, his eyes staring into goodness knows where. And when we were having sex, that newfound savagery went from being a novelty to hurting me. He once bit me too deeply: the wound needed stitches. At home, I lied and said a dog had done it. The boy's family took him to one doctor after another, one psychiatrist after another, but nothing worked. The poor thing began to fade away. They finally had him committed to a nearby mental hospital, the White Hart. I was convinced it had all been due to my father's eyes, to his damned venom.

Who could have wanted to bring such a curse into the world? To leave people their bodies but without the means to use them. Incapable bodies, but with the full memory of once having had those means. The full sense of past powers lost in inexplicable bodies. Like Jesús, my sweetheart ended in the body of something always considered inferior, savage.

Witchcraft, that's what they said. They told my mother it might even have been someone close to the family, someone very close, someone the family knew well, and that the spell couldn't be reversed and might even be contagious or hereditary. Why my father? What had he done? No one knew. They didn't know (if they admitted that such a thing was in fact possible) from what form of jealousy or rage it arose.

For a while, my mother attempted to discover who was behind it all, but she started to forget when other problems of, shall we say, greater density came along; more comprehensible, less unlikely problems. Hunger.

That was when my mother decided to leave town. And that's why I know nothing more about my father.

When I was small, despite seeing my mother constantly weeping about my father's desertion, everything was simpler: love was when she invited sumptuously dressed, exotic people from faraway places to our home. I'd spend hours under the table, listening to their conversation. Her hair would be piled up high and she'd hold her glass between her proudly displayed slender fingers. There would be liqueurs, which she'd sometimes let me taste from a little finger discreetly placed below the table for me to suck. Then I'd go back to my place, occasionally glancing at those men and women who spoke delicious languages. Seated at the head of the table, my mother was flattered by their comments. See, María, she'd say, lifting the cloth to look at me, these men think I'm beautiful, amusing, elegant. I guess I'll marry one of them so he can be your father. And I'd nod and ask for a little more of the sweet liqueur she dipped her finger in for me to suck. Eventually, drowsy from the alcohol, I'd flop out along a row of chairs and when I came to—however hard she tried to wake me earlier—the delicacies and the love were gone. And when the delicacies were gone, my mother went back to being her usual self. She'd say: Are you still here, María? I thought you were dead. Or my tipsy mother would pretend she didn't know me. In the protection of a corner of our apartment, she lost all her hostess's elegance. Who are you? she'd shout. Go away! I'd try to keep her company, because I knew she was frightened, but she'd push me away and I'd sometimes fall flat on my face or on my butt.

She'd repeat: Who are you? What planet are you from?

I began to think that I, María, really did come from another world, that I, María, was a dead girl, a ghost terrifying my mother. Years passed before I understood that those guests, those spectacular female friends of my mother, those princely prospective fathers, didn't exist. Their mouths adorned with neat mustaches, their sumptuous, perfectly plucked eyebrows, their deep-set, black eyes, their languages, their clothes: none of it was real. But I've never been able to explain why, if they didn't exist, I remember them.

As I grew older, love made me more and more unhappy; it was a war I waged the way you shoulder a dark secret. My first love, my friend, my first and only lover until that time, had turned into a savage being who stared out the window, under the influence of those pills that made him fat and left his wits dulled. I only visited him once, and never went back. I couldn't bear the smell of bleach and urine mixed with the odor of his growing fur.

Sometimes, late at night, when I was unable to stop thinking about him or shake off those thoughts, I'd go to my mother's bedroom to watch her sleeping, to surprise myself by the consolation it gave me to feel the way I felt imagining she was dead. This is true love, I'd think, like a sort of heat that flares up again when confronted with the possibility of loss.

After a while, weary of sobbing, I'd put my hand by her nostrils and when I felt her breath, I'd tiptoe back to my room to wait for the sun to rise.

That's why I tried to explain things to Salvador: when two people really love and communicate with each other, they represent complementary parts of the same thing. You're the circumference, I'm the empty space inside the circle. When I saw Salvador with that woman, I saw chaos. A circle that was losing its circumference, a circle that was merging into everything outside and becoming nothing. I saw the flesh, just the flesh. I felt trapped, asphyxiated by that woman's mass of color, by her smell, a pair of enormous breasts coming to kill me. In the middle of all the chaos, the notion of her body was taking root inside me, it was like a kind of rage, of fire, like a kind of fish that cuts a groove through the water. Everything inside me ached. In my memory, that body was reduced to a back, the buttocks, and the swaying breasts, a body shining in the blue morning light of a polluted city. It was the best body in the world, a body that left the competition standing. What hope had I? I knew the deed was done, it had happened: when I saw them, something fell out of joint or the pieces finally fit together. I knew perfectly well what it meant. It was him with another woman and things were exactly what they seemed. They always had been, I was right, the whole universe was telling me so. Nobody would contradict me now: he was capable of loving another woman; loving her body at least, of feeling a desire for her that was more enduring, more complex than any affection.

Afterwards, I thought that when he was speaking to me he was in fact seeing her. When he said: If I touch your skin this way, so softly, almost using only my nails, I feel this is a memory, that we aren't here and this isn't our real body; when I saw his eyes glaze, claiming that he was thinking of us, I knew it wasn't us he was thinking of.

For him, I was a chest of drawers where the house keys were hidden. And she was the house with its picture windows, its doors and hallways. There could be no doubt that she was more beautiful, more desirable, more intelligent, I thought. If that weren't true, why was he doing this to me?

Why are you doing this to me! I screamed as I watched them, but only a whisper emerged from my throat. I turned my back and, allowing myself to be torn apart by my wails, packed a bag with my most important things and left the house without saying a word. A few steps from the gate, I looked back and, seeing him naked in the doorway, his mouth filled with an unutterable scream, I started to run and he, as if unaware of his nudity, chased me.

That night, I hid in the countryside and around the place I found to sit—the trunk of a felled tree—I had the feeling that the conifers were looking at me. Hey there, girl, they said. Do you realize you're ill? Take some of our leaves and chew them, then rub the paste on your temples and genitals; that might cure you. I couldn't believe it. I started running again and then a flashlight shone in my face. Blinded, I turned back toward the darkness, so careless of what my body was doing that I tumbled onto the leaves before the astonished gazes of the conifers, which were like elegant men in suits.

I've found you, María, said Salvador, who was pinning me down under his now-clothed body.

I've found you, María. No one will ever mean as much to me as you do, no one, ever, I promise you, María.

"Why?" asks Elvira as the man prepares the rope, and during a pause in the ceremony, she lights her cigarette.

"Why I want to kill myself? I don't want things to go on being real just because I perceive them."

"What things?"

"Feelings, for instance, or pictures, letters, memories, rocks laid and forgotten. At the moment of death, in an awareness of pain, the universe . . . the world of viruses . . . things in general. Do you understand?"

"I once tried to put an end to my life too, because it just caused me pain and revolted me . . . A certain person had forced me into oblivion. Someone who merely had to smile his smile once too often. By pure chance, believe it or not, however incredible it may sound, my life was saved. My ego was forced to learn to put up with me, to bear the unbearable."

The man, who is black, readies the rope in the darkened room where Elvira's spangled shoes provide the only glimmer of light. His skin is so dark that whenever he speaks, it's as if the deep shadows of that basement were uttering the words.

"The negation of the will to exist is a bold affirmation of the will. The suicide wants life, and simply rejects the conditions under which he experiences it."

I know that Elvira overcomes her will to follow him into death and, without turning her head, watches the man stand on the chair: "I think you'd better do it now," she tells him, and by the rapid blinking of her eyes, she obviously hears the sharp crack of a neck breaking.

My fantasy was constructed around that scene from a movie. Stringing up a rope, putting an end to it all. With Salvador watching. Salvador resisting the urge to follow me into death. My fantasy was constructed around his pain: if he loves someone else, the space of my death would take over that place, it would fill everything to the brim; my absence would restore my body to his memory and would occupy the whole of his mind.

One day, after we'd abandoned my father, some men turned up and, even though I was in my teens by then, they carried me in their arms from my mother's house, and, even though she was capable of walking, they put her in a wheelchair. And then they locked her up in the White Hart. The neighbors had realized she was schizophrenic. I've never visited her. I'm frightened by the idea of having to see her; frightened she'll make me believe all over again that I'm dead. It took me a long time to recognize that this body is indeed here, that the flesh I'm composed of exists. I don't want to destroy this body now it's finally mine. I'm curious about the future, and that curiosity is my true survival instinct. I have to admit I hadn't recognized that until I was perceived by Salvador. It wasn't hard, he had this thing about smells and smelled me as if he were breathing me in, he touched me as if I were the last real thing in the world. That's not true now. But back then, in the beginning, we even had the same dreams. One night I dreamed someone was knocking at my door and when I opened it, he was there, and since then he's been able to pass from his dreams into mine.

All the magic finally disappeared when I saw him with that woman. I was so exhausted after I fled the house that I had a siesta and Salvador came into my dream, but there was also a man dressed in white, and I thought he was a nurse and was going to carry me away in his arms, and outside I'd see my mother in her wheelchair, but in an instant the man stopped being a man and became that thing with hundreds of eyes encrusted all around its body. One eye opened and three closed, two closed and five opened . . . I can't recall its shape; it could as easily have been a huge dark mass, a little man, or a dog. That thing was probably a mix of all the animals we combine in dreams. It came, stayed a day with us, looked at us with those hundreds of bright stars, and then we were never again able to dream as we used to.

Due to that same pain, the first visions appeared and began to unravel real events.

One day in the pool, a giant swimmer cast a shadow below my minute body.

That thing down there isn't me, I thought; I'm much smaller. And while I was dressing, a woman sitting in the semi-dark in a corner asked me: Did you see that really skinny woman? Didn't she look like a cat fetus under the water?

She was talking about me, talking about me, but when I turned my head in search of her face, I could tell the voice wasn't hers: the steam filling the room was addressing me, trying to get inside my ear, whispering to me.

Another day, on my way home, I stopped outside an old hotel I'd never noticed before. I went in. I tend to feel curious about places that are always closed and if the doors are ever left open, I enter; that's what happens with churches and old houses, and it happened with that hotel.

In the first hallway, the one leading to the stairs, there was a man curled up in a ball. I watched him for a long time, trying to figure out if he was dead, then a woman passed by and walked right over him without noticing that he moaned as her heels dug in. One heel landed on his forehead and he brushed it away, so I was able to see that he was alive and had long, really long, grimy nails. The woman fell over and immediately rubbed her knees. When I saw the blood, I ran to help her. Señora, I said, you can't complain, that poor man was only trying to stop you from stepping on his face. She had already gone up a couple of stairs, but turned to say: What man?

She looked at me the way my mother sometimes did and continued on her way.

When I turned around to check on the man, he'd disappeared.

Another day, a boy with fire-red hair was crossing the street at the same time as me. It was like seeing blue roses. *Blue roses don't exist in nature.* So boys with fire-red hair can't exist in nature either. He was like a reluctant albino who's decided to have the impenetrable white of his hair dyed red. He was like a burning match head or a live coal held up to the wind in the middle of the street. I could feel the heat coming from his youthful head and wanted to see his face, to ascertain that someone like that could exist and walk around as if it were the most normal thing in the world. I tried to cut across in front of him, but he kept turning his back to me, I walked discreetly around his body, but he kept turning to his friends, and when I swiveled around, I only managed to see the scruff of his neck. As it was a public holiday, a lot was going on in the city and there were so many people in the street that I thought I could hide in someone to get a look at him, but was unwilling to start the madwoman's dance. He'll realize, I thought. A young man like that, so tall, so muscular . . . a blue rose, no doubt about it. That boy must be the Devil or something that doesn't belong in this world. Otherwise, why didn't he just stop and show me his face? Why was he so keen not to be discovered? He probably doesn't have a face, I concluded. He was moving on with the confidence of an old man who has managed to retain his youth, his fame, and has firm, well-toned muscles beneath his skin. Because no one under fifty walks that way. I wanted to see his face, wanted to know who he was, what he was doing. I speeded up to reach him but he was caught up in a surge of people. Suddenly, someone stuck out their foot and I tripped and I rolled over and over downhill. The street was on a steep slope, the street had turned into a long slide down which I alone and none of the other bodies who'd been walking beside me slid. As I rolled, I thought I'd surely break my bones but I felt nothing besides a profound sense of regret, a great many bottled-up tears in my solar plexus, breathlessness. Help, someone help me, I need help. Nobody so much as looked around. The sun was scorching. My face was elongating and I could hear the hairs of my eyebrows burning. When I opened my eyes, he was there: my father. That hair reflected the sun like a polished coin. His hair had always been so white, so really white that when he lit a cigarette, the flame would tinge it red.

Father, aren't you dead? I asked, and he lunged at my face, his teeth bared.

When I woke, Salvador's eyes were weighing down on me again. Salvador, I said, when you see I'm having a nightmare, wake me, don't just lie there watching, please, for God's sake, wake me. I was bathed in my own tears. Just how damned long have you been watching me?

He said nothing, just got out of bed and went to the bathroom, shutting himself in there for hours.

On the other side of the door, I could hear him whistling a merry tune.

I've told you before, Salvador: My home, you're my home. You're my safe haven, a place where there's always a warm fire. I've realized something: the other day I thought your right hand was my left one, and sometimes, when I see you through the glass door, I think you're my reflection. It sets my head in a whirl. What would happen if you really were me? I feel like something would slip out of joint, something important. A great rock would crash down on a city or hundreds of new animals would emerge from the water. We're losing our minds, Salvador, I think we have to leave. We need to leave very soon. I know you're going to agree because I always know what you're thinking. I urgently need to get out of here, let's take a trip, go to the desert, nothing ever happens there, we'll take provisions, stop off at the supermarket, buy canned stuff and lots of water. It'll be an adventure. It'll be lovely. You know, the clear desert landscape, a different sort of air. I don't like the city anymore, I'm getting to hate it.

That's what I said.

I could smell every morsel of his guilt. I said it all from outside the bathroom so I didn't have to meet his eyes. When he came out, he had no option but to say yes and then, with our backs turned to each other, we packed a few things and filled water bottles.

The sight of him, so unhappy about our departure, made something disintegrate inside me. I felt like reality was a piece of fine gauze in which, after millennia of being stroked by a sharp edge, a hole had appeared and that hole was enlarging and swallowing us.

SALVADOR

During the night I heard my name and thought she was calling me. It was a voice like the sound of wind in the trees. I got up and went to her room. María preferred us to sleep in separate beds. She said that being apart would help us recover our own, independent dreams. For years, I visited her every night and she visited me, and even then we were together; in our dreams, that is. I don't know how it started; one night I dreamed I was knocking at a door and she opened it and since then we've been able to cross over into each other's dreams. At first I found being seen by her even in that private cranny of sleep somehow promiscuous, but to be honest it felt like I was penetrating her more deeply than this small piece of my body ever could. It was like a yearning being fulfilled, with the sensation that we were finally becoming one. The anguish of separation: reduced. And we played in the dreams. Particularly at hybridizing animals: I'd show her a whale and in a flash she'd add the legs of a gazelle. And, yes, the whale would be able to stand upright.

When I got to her bedside, my name was no longer sounding. Everything was in silence. She was curled up, her head buried under the pillow. She turned to me with her eyes closed and said: I'll eat myself.

She'd bitten her tongue in her sleep and, when she woke, was horrified to find herself spitting blood, and the only thing she said that whole day was my name: Salvador.

The great magic of divination possibly consists of interpreting things so nuanced that the relationship between them would pass unnoticed by anyone but a sorcerer. It's said that if you happen to meet someone and the two of you begin to try to figure out the connections, it's possible to identify one person or place without which that convergence would never have occurred. That's magic. It was something like that with María. More than that. Everything that happened before we met prepared our encounter. Something strange, like the origins of my own birth.

It all began when my mother fell in love with and married my father, who was forty years older than her. He was a cultivated man, an avid reader; he was always carrying some heavy tome and instructing people, and I know that due to his solitariness, he'd had various lives: he'd been a teacher, a soldier, a farmhand, and did other jobs I never knew about; my mother thought he'd even been a hired killer in his early life.

She was hardly out of childhood when they met. I know he did wait for her, for one or two years anyway, him trying to make her understand the nature of desire and her trying to get her head around the idea that he'd introduce his heap of flesh into the orifice that she'd only ever thought of as the opening in her body through which urine came out. That's how young my mother was and how little she knew about herself.

Why had they gotten married? She was a very poor orphan, the silent girl who served coffee in the house of one of his business partners. What kind of business? I don't know. We never talked about that. They had to marry so he could get her out of there. I'm not sure exactly how long they waited after they first saw each other, but I know it wasn't long. He took her to live with him, taught her to read, showed her illustrated books about the amatory arts so that she'd eventually let him have his way, but she wasn't interested. She wanted to sit under the orange trees, playing with the insects and planting flowers. She was able to grow flowers that weren't even suited to the soil and climate of the town. In other gardens, the same flowers were scorched by the frost.

My father finally gave up teaching her the things he wanted her to know for his own benefit and resigned himself to telling her the stories my mother stored up. So, rather than a father figure, I grew up with the stories that father had told, because by the time I'd have been capable of having a proper conversation with him, he was dead.

My mother didn't understand the wall of maps he used to spend hours sitting before, she didn't understand the correspondence with friends she never met, and didn't even know where the letters were written from or why. She didn't understand the long periods he spent in the spartan room where he slept separately from her, but she did sometimes go in there to shave him, and then they talked. In exchange, when he finally came out, he'd bring her seeds and tell her the stories that she in turn told me, adding screams and special effects. If he told a story with horses, she'd rap her fingertips on the table and neigh. If it was a horror story, she screamed.

All the stories were about my father's multiple lives.

I know my father had a son, a man who must have been a lot older than my mother. I know he turned up one day and asked to be invited in, but my mother said no, and that was the only time I heard her refuse a person entry. Who is he? I asked, and she said: Your brother. Nobody mentioned the visit again.

No, I hadn't known that I had a brother until that day. I was always alone. I thought I'd have liked to play with him, get to know him and become his friend. I imagined him as a second father, perhaps because I understood that mine was ageing fast. From the time I came to know him, I was certain that my father's body would start to decompose long before his death, and that's how it was: he was plummeting earthward. The very weight of his sparse flesh indicated the road ahead: he gradually became more hunched, smaller; it seemed like at any minute his face would come up against his knees and then, with the dark, wrinkly texture of the very last apple on the tree, he'd clutch his shins and die.

That's why I wanted to meet my brother. And that's why I went to talk to my father. He explained the situation:

I slept with that woman once. I can't give you any further details, but I can say that it was a mistake, a terrible mistake. She got pregnant. She used to meet other men on the sly. I know, because I spied on her one night from a tree and saw her flesh glinting in the streetlight under the body of someone else.

But the child was mine, I'm sure of that. He looks just like me; we're like two peas in a pod. But you can't get to know him, it would only do you harm.

After that, I said nothing more about my brother. After that, my mother was killed. After my mother died, my father followed her. Then María and I met.

I'm not complaining: that's the timeline of my life.

María never learned how to be with other people. She used to say that just as soon as she started to do it with someone, she felt deeply nostalgic and wouldn't be able to continue. She said that even when she was with another person she felt that it was really me, and then all the excitement of cheating evaporated, and with it her libido. She also told me that when she was with other men, she thought too much and while they were trying to satisfy her, she'd be making a shopping list or recalling movies she'd watched. She was obsessed, for instance, by a scene where a soldier is spinning around in one of those contraptions magicians and fakirs strap people to and then throw knives around them. She said the nearest thing to pleasure she experienced was when she managed to remember that scene perfectly: the soldier stops turning so that the villain can inject him with a truth serum. The soldier (who, it goes without saying, is the good guy) goes on turning while the serum pours into his bloodstream and when its venom takes effect, the baddie, just to torture him, asks: "What do you fear most in the world?" And the soldier replies: "The possibility that love is not enough."

She tried sleeping with other men because I'd fallen in love with someone else, or at least I thought I had. In bed, everything was wonderful with my new lover and I had to tell María that, because it's the truth: you get nostalgic sometimes. Especially when there's temporal contiguity between one encounter and the other. There were times when I'd come to María's body, wanting her more than anyone else, but everything in me was seeped in the body of the other person. Even when I was speaking, certain tones of voice or pronunciation errors that weren't mine would give me away. And I'd see my desire fade away in the face of guilt.

And then I'm constantly surprised by certain differences in people's bodies. No, I don't mean "beauty," I'm talking about something else. I mean that in the darkness, your hand reaches out and touches an orifice, touches it until it becomes wet and then a spiral opens up, a spiral that's drawing you toward it, as if it were an ocean whirlpool—yes, that's it—and you're sucked into it like you're travelling inside yourself, in your own warm blood, your pulsing blood, all the blood in that specific piece of you sinking into the loop of someone who's opening her legs to you and you feel as though you've always been a small boat with a sleeper at the tiller and there's nothing left to do but go along with the drift.

Then I think, two whirlpools, three whirlpools, four whirlpools, the differences between them.

But no, I'm lying when I say that too. Sometimes you don't look at her, you don't see the spiral. And to be honest, sometimes you enter there just to get your fill. Something inside you says: Yes, you can, let's go there. I don't need it, but I want it.

The body is sometimes like those people who have experienced hunger in the past and force their children to finish every scrap on their plates.

When I saw my mother dead, her skirt was covering her face and beside her, as if a part of her body, I could see the head of her injured dog. It had been stabbed from various angles, its muzzle was slashed and a few teeth were visible. We weren't able to save it, but I'm certain it wouldn't have wanted to be saved. Because that dog loved my mother truly. It loved my mother, or owed more to her than to me or my father.

She'd helped that dog to thrive too.

It was a bug-faced, male dog that had been left at the door as a puppy. Ugly though it was, she'd taken it in; she wrapped it in a small blanket, cuddled it like a child and gave it what should have been my milk; all the while sitting under the orange tree, as if showing off her newborn. It was something to see her, with the creature on her lap, holding the feeding bottle of warm milk at an angle under a tree heavy with juicy, yellow, round fruit. And the smell, such a smell. A specific smell, like wet cardstock and rain falling to earth. That could only be the smell of orange trees, and my mother there with her dog, damp with the droplets of milk falling on its fur. When the neighbors who were always making fun of her approached, pretending to be there to say good day, they'd uncover the puppy's face and go from cooing to irritating bursts of laughter, and then coarse insults. You could see they were basically scared. My mother wouldn't so much as move a muscle; she sat there quietly, gazing at her dog's two patches of yellow fur that she always called its "real eyes." I'd watch her as I crawled around, occasionally eating a few ants.

I remember that at the far end of our small garden there were some new orange trees. To me they seemed enormous, but they were only recently planted. I learned to stand upright by clutching their growing trunks. I'd support myself on the earth, which was always moist, and with that fresh and, for a baby, heavy feel on my hands, I'd gradually raise myself up.

María went to work in a sort of morgue. It's something she doesn't like to talk about. I remember she once told me a story and it's not just that I happen to remember that story; I can't forget it. She said that on her first day, she was asked to dress a corpse. They explained how to sit up a body with rigor mortis to put a shirt on it, but when the moment came, she couldn't. The body fell on top of her and the stiffness holding all the muscles together prevented her from even straightening the arms to put them into the sleeves. She said she tried, but exhausted by the weight of the corpse, she burst into tears and the man in the blue gown, after a long harangue, said: See here, María, there are a whole heap of bodies in this place belonging to people who suffered a great deal when they were alive; their families—if they have any—have been looking for them for a long time—if they looked for them at all. This is their last journey and it's our job to give them a decent send-off, so if this body won't allow itself to be dressed, talk to it. Tell it that it's here now, it's been found, there's nothing to worry about any longer.

She said that the man in the blue gown went over to the corpse María was supposed to dress and put his mouth to the purplish ear.

Let me dress you, you've reached the end of your journey, tomorrow you can rest. Let yourself be dressed so people can pray for you.

María looked on as the corpse seemed to relax and the man dressed it with no trouble at all.

While my mother was removing the dripping seeds from a piece of fruit that had fallen from the tree, she said to me: When you do things with love, they turn out well. I didn't know if she was alluding to her fruit or me. And it wasn't until much later that I understood it was also an allusion to my half brother. He hadn't "turned out well" according to my mother. She said those words a few days after the strange visit.

My mother went on removing the seeds from that piece of fruit, her fingers covered in a red liquid that turned purple when mixed with spittle or water. Then she said: Your father must have told you, Salvador, that when you were still in my belly, I used to go out to play with the local boys. One day, the little brothers of the oldest boys joined us and I went to sit with them on the sidewalk. I was tired; I didn't know you were inside me and didn't understand why I felt so odd when I was kicking a ball around. The young boys began asking where I came from and what my parents were called. They thought your father was my father. Even though we don't look the least alike! They asked why my eyes didn't slant at the corners, said it was like someone had taken a knife to make them wider on each side. I said that was how the people of my breed were and they started to laugh, tapping their bellies. Breed is for puppies, they told me. Then they asked other things, but I was watching a boy kicking the ball into our goal and when I turned back to them, the boys were discussing something they didn't explain to me. I asked them what they were talking about and they said: Nothing, we're chatting to the little one. What little one? And one of them pointed at my belly and said: That one.

She liked removing the seeds from pomegranates; she'd scoop the pith that holds the seeds from the husk and eat it. The pith is bitter, Salvador, but it will do you good. And she'd put it all in a glass so I'd want to eat it. Come on, Salvador, eat up, it's good for you now the cold weather is coming. And then she went on: Your father will have told you that when those children said that to me, I took no notice. I went on playing, running hither and thither, but then one night when I was in bed, I heard something beating. It was beating so strongly, Salvador. Ba boom, ba boom, the whole room was full of the noise. And I wanted to call someone to tell me they could hear it too, but I was alone and no one came. And then you spoke, I heard you speak in a voice that reminded me of when we used to lower my brothers to the bottom of the well to collect the last of the water and they'd shout from down there when they wanted us to pull up the rope. I was really scared and ran out of the house before I could figure out what you were saying to me. Outside, perched in the pomegranate tree, I saw an owl, and the owl was singing. I was frightened to death and raced to the town to tell an old woman and she said: Why did you tell me that, woman? Your son was going to be a shaman, a sorcerer, he was going to have special powers, but for that to come true you had to keep the secret. But now you've told me, you'll have a normal child, like any other.

That's what my mother said while I was popping those seeds in their red juice with my teeth. When I'd finished, I remember I was close to tears and threatened to throw the glass down so that she'd pick me up. She came over and, to distract me, put a finger to her lips and took me silently to see a bird with a blue breast that never sang.

It was María who decided we had to come to the desert. Why not take a few months to be nobody? she suggested. She'd had enough of living in the same place for so long. All we do is be together, Salvador; I feel like I only exist for you. She hugged me so tightly I had an intuition that the journey would be a dreadful idea. Yet I agreed, I needed to get away too.

I want to find out how someone who knows nothing about me sees me, she said, we're so used to each other that I'm already certain you'll say yes.

In silence, after that implicit affirmation, we packed, filled our water bottles, and the following morning got into the car.

I needed to get away. I'd met Daniela and things had ended badly. It wasn't the first occasion I'd cheated on María, but this time it had all gotten out of hand. María had seen us together. When I raised my eyes from below Daniela's undulating body, I saw her in the doorway, her eyes brimming with tears. I don't know how long she'd been there; long enough to see the moles on my lover's shoulders and butt, and to see me, red, aroused, sweating, on the point of crying out. She'd had time to compare her body with Daniela's and, although she'd only seen it from behind, she'd tried to check if her breasts were firm or sagging as she moved.

When I saw her, with that look of being sunk in sorrow, I pushed Daniela off and, just like in a telenovela, ran out after

María, who had walked away at the slow pace of defeat. Then she saw me at the gate and started running down the street, and I lost sight of her as she turned the corner. For a few moments, I ran after her, but when I realized I was in the buff, I returned to the bedroom, where Daniela was still waiting for me.

Are you crazy, honey? she asked as I approached the bed. Her naked body gave off the smell of blood and coconut. Where did you go?

I had no answer to that question and simply asked her to dress and leave my home. Are you kicking me out? she asked, banging her boots against the wall. I had no answer to that question either. I stood there in silence as she stuffed her brassiere in her purse and hurriedly buttoned her blouse. Her nipples were still erect and the blouse was so tight her sweat soaked through it. She only had her boots to put on, but I urgently needed her out. Daniela, please leave my home, I repeated. What happened, Salvador? Can you just tell me what happened? She pleaded with me to tell it as if I were sorting out some problem at work, in that same happy-to-help telephone operator voice. Dammit, Daniela, go to hell, just get out of here you bitch. I grabbed her arm and dragged her out of the house. Then, through the spyhole, I watched her lean against the wall and push her feet into her boots. Daniela was crying too; her eyes were lighter when she cried. Making two women cry in one day is bad karma, I thought. I went back to our bed—María's and mine—straightened the sheets, sprayed perfume on them and called her thirty-four times. She didn't answer. She's had enough, I thought. She won't come back this time. I'm a fool, a damn fool.

My father wasn't a faithful man, that was the only thing we never had any doubts about. I didn't understand how, being so old, he could cheat on my mother, who was a lovely, dark-haired woman with long, black lashes. Or why anyone would look twice at that stooped man; he never mentioned how old he was, but it was easy to guess that the years ran to many dozens. He already looked elderly to me when I had to follow him to the bar and sit there with him until one of us fell asleep and the other took him home.

My mother made me follow him; it gave me a feeling of strength when she said I had to be there to stop anyone punching him. To be honest, my mother was afraid he'd leave her for another woman. That never happened, the man soon got very old and the time he squandered on women was spent being alone. He'd shut himself away in his room, with the walls covered with books, maps, and the names of saints, and stay in there for days.

After my mother's death, my father died. The old man was lying there one morning with his mouth open. I remember I hadn't before noticed that he'd lost all his teeth. At first I was afraid he'd been killed by the same person who'd done for my mother, but then I realized it was just old age. The day before his death, however, my father had looked radiant, more radiant than ever before. And then I was able to get a glimpse of why women adored him and I wanted with all my might to grow up to be like him. That day, his face seemed much younger and his eyes shone. The only things that gave away my father's real age were his hands: the veins stood out like black roots and there was dark grime under his uncut nails.

I didn't bury my father. I asked for him to be cremated and kept the urn containing his ashes in my living room.

When María said let's get out of here, the first thing I took was his ashes.

I'd have liked to say: I think he'd have wanted his ashes to be scattered in the desert. I'd have liked to believe that such a purely sentimental gesture would make her forgive me for everything, that she'd put her arms around me from behind, kiss the nape of my neck, and say: We'll take them with us then.

Going away with her was the only thing I could do to make up for all my attempted betrayals. I love you, María, I said when I eventually found her. She was hiding in a park, crying her eyes out. I said: No one will ever mean as much to me as you do, no one, ever, María. I swear it.

Fine, she said, absently, and that was just about all she said that day; she spent the rest of the afternoon staring at the flowers in a planter, watering them, moving them into the sun, removing the dried edges from the leaves.

Then she came out with that stuff about getting away. I could read in her mind that she meant getting away from Daniela, getting as far away as possible from that dumb woman, but what she said was: I've had enough of all this.

That night, in her sleep, she said: I'll eat myself.

I didn't tell her what I'd dreamed: her voice—something like the sound the wind makes when it's carrying those thick layers of sand from the desert—was calling my name. I was in our small garden and went to look for her inside the house; her voice had faded, but I knew she was there. María? She didn't answer, but I could hear her breathing as if through a speaker. Her respiration was distorted by some strange filter, it was like high-volume white noise. Painful to hear. María? She didn't answer. The furniture in the house was different; the light was different. The sun was weirdly bright. Then I spotted her turning to go into our bedroom, I knew she was naked because I managed to get a glance of her hair falling over the small of her back.

Time after time I moved toward her, and time after time I only saw her turn, and that moment stretched out and we circled so often that I had the sensation of being on a carousel and falling off.

María? I called again before finally finding her. She was on her bed and her sweaty body was enclosed by another sweating body. What are you doing, María? She didn't hear me, just went on moaning and breathing while that man, that being, moved his body to between her legs. She moved as though she'd always been making love with him that way. I'm not sure what gave them that air, but they seemed eternal.

María, why are you doing this to me? I cried.

They say this man was lightning in a past life, she told me. And then she added: Anyway, why are you still here when you don't love me?

That was when I woke. María was staring at me.

Why did you do that to me? she asked. I don't know how long she'd been crying, but her eyes looked small and the lids red and swollen.

I think I love her, I said.

One day, I asked who God was and where he lived and my father took down the heavy tome he was always reading. He read aloud one or two phrases, gesturing with his hands, and then pushed me out of his room. Leave him alone, child, your father doesn't want anyone to distract him from seeing God, said my mother, and then took me outside to look at the bugs that had attached themselves to the oranges.

When I was little, I used to pray to my parents' love, because I believed it was like a God. But then, as happens to everyone, disbelief came along. I began to see that my mother was absurdly devoted to a man about whom she knew nothing more than the stories he told. And those stories . . . those stories can't be true. For instance, he was always talking about someone he'd met in the desert, I don't know what my father was doing in the desert, but he was there during the war, always covering his own rear. He was riding his black horse, when he came across a trader whose mule had died. Jump up here, my father said, and I'll take you to where you can get a new animal. And the man had mounted behind him.

The way he told it, with his eyes lost in the distance, night had fallen when the trader said: I'll get down here, and I'll go the way of gold, which always returns, Vicente. If gold is buried, it unburies itself, and sometimes if you share it around, it multiplies. Take this gold coin for your help, and let's hope it can do the same for you as you did for me: speed me a little on my way. May this carry you faster to your destination, and may all of your line know true love, if the Lord so wills it. It's been a great pleasure.

With a grand flourish, the trader deposited the gold coin in my father's hand and retreated, making a small bow with each step.

Who are you? asked my father. That coin will tell you, said the trader, then, in a mocking tone, he growled like a dog at my father and disappeared alone into the darkness of the valley.

When we found my mother dead, that coin was right there in the deepest of her wounds, as if someone had forced it in.

I saw the coin, all covered in blood, and I saw my mother and the dog lying there, but I didn't cry, didn't do anything. I went to bed because I was feeling weary. I'm very tired, I said, and then I slept for days. When I woke, my mother was in a box, surrounded by women dressed in black who made me look at her.

It was about that time that my father said to me: It's a curse, and has to be a sin for a woman to die before her husband.

After that he spent his days sitting in the shade of the orange tree, staring at that coin.

I don't know what the coin was doing there, I thought it was lost, mused my father day after day. And each evening, after saying that, he'd fetch a wooden stool and polish the coin, over and over, as if he'd never get the dirt out. He sent me to the creek for bucket after bucket of water, sent me for soapwort, and bleach, but in his eyes the coin was never clean. It even seemed as though he were no longer trying to clean it, but to make it disappear. And the coin shone like the sun.

Why did my mom have that thing in the wound that killed her? I asked. And he told me the story of the trader he'd met by the side of the road.

I dreamed again last night, I say.

I was sitting in our small garden, on a tiny child's chair, but this time, María, it wasn't you who called to me; I was saying my own name. I got out of the chair, looked up to the sky, and the sun was a gold coin. The light it emitted was like the light of a mirror, and it made small black and white spots appear before my eyes. Slightly blinded, I went inside the house. I could still hear myself saying my own name. María? You didn't reply. I was afraid, but for no specific reason, and that was worse: it was pure, unadulterated fear and it spread, leaving its mark on everything. I could feel it in my whole body, forcing my muscles to contract horribly. My toenails dug into my shoes, I couldn't stop them, it seemed like if I tried to walk any other way, I'd fall. Stooping, with my fingers bent inward, I felt like a monkey. I felt like the fear had always been present, just growing until it took over completely. María? You didn't answer. You weren't there, and it felt as though you never had been. With my whole body tensed in horror, I looked like a savage animal, I remember thinking in the dream: If anyone sees me this way, they'll be startled, so I mustn't let anyone ever see me in this state. I called you again, and again, walking through every room in the house. My voice had stopped hearing itself and when I reached the bedroom—the place I'd left until last to search—I saw someone sleeping in the bed. María? I pulled back the sheets to uncover you, thinking how lovely it would be to lie beside your warm body and embrace you. You'd half wake and say, as you always do: Everything okay? And I'd say: Yes, everything's fine, the sun is weird. I'd wait until you were fully awake to tell you about the fear I'd felt, even though there, at that moment, lying beside you, it would be a comfort to hear your breathing, I'd massage your breasts and you'd take my hand to pull me closer, María. But when I lifted the sheet, you weren't there; I was looking at myself. I was asleep, but the light streaming below the sheet woke me and I stared into my eyes.

María? María, are you listening? I'm telling you about my dream, it's fascinating, but you're not paying attention.

Ah, María answers.

She's in the front passenger seat and her hair is flying loose through the window. You're not listening to me, not paying attention, I think, but I don't say so. María is miles away, but there are moments when some force changes her expression and it seems as though she's in possession of some great certainty. In those moments, she speaks, saying practical things: she reads me a list of provisions to take to the desert. Don't forget to stop at the supermarket, Salvador. We need water, canned food, and toilet paper, of course, that's so important.

Before going in, she says goodbye with a kiss on my lips and another on my forehead and laughs in her childishly affectionate way. I say: You're crazy, but she can't hear me by then. I watch her pass the security guard and the glass door opens before her.

It's hot, I've been driving for hours, my butt hurts, there's some strange bitterness rising from my stomach. I haven't felt hungry the whole day and the diaphanous flames thrown up by the road surface have been making me feel nauseous. I want to sleep.

Just like in those dreams where you're about to open a letter that contains a secret—the name of God, or the reason you ended up in this world—she told me she'd dreamed of a person she was madly in love with. Somebody whose reach was almost infinite and whose face was impossible to see. She told me that in the dream she was running around his body but her field of vision was always limited to his back and shoulders, never his face. He and I were together, looking into the void, and he was standing there beside me with no face, she said. And one day, with those bright eyes women have when they fall in love, she also said: I know you're that person, Salvador, I'm certain.

Although it's night, the heat is still boiling my brains when I wake, but the inferno has died down a little. Where can María have gotten to? It's hours since she went in to buy water and toilet paper. I stretch, massage my temples. There's a heavy feel to the air, it's hard to breathe. She was most likely hungry, got tired of watching me sleep and went to find something to eat.

An idea pops into my mind, the remote possibility that she might have left me. The food is the only good thing in this place. It's devilishly hot. I hope the tires don't burst. Some ideas wall in others, my palms are sweating but it feels cold because, outside the car, the heat thrown up from the asphalt makes everything seem like a huge grill. I walk to the stalls surrounding the supermarket, a complex of guy ropes and awnings. She's not there, María is nowhere to be seen. A woman this tall with hair this long. No? Are you sure? I go to the next stall, the people reply unwillingly. The cold sweat has spread across my whole back. Temples, massage your temples, everything will be fine. Where can the woman have gotten to?

What's she like? someone asks. And then I shout: She's a woman, for God's sake! How difficult can it be to find a woman this tall, with hair this long, and a face that's nothing like yours, you dogface son of a fucking whore! The man has gotten to his feet, his fists at the ready, and I hurry away. What have I done? I need to calm down. Breathe a little, find María. She can't have left you, she wouldn't do that. She loves you, she told you that you were The Man. You're never going to find anything else like this. Where can she have gotten to? María, shout. María, come on out, I call, as if we were playing hide-and-seek. The diners in the complex of yellow awnings laugh. What's up with that man, Mom? asks a little boy and his mother whispers in his ear. You can all go to hell, I think. I'll return to the car and there she'll be, leaning against the door, tidying her hair in the rear-view mirror. She'll say: Ah, you're back, I've been looking for you, and I'll embrace her like she's never been embraced before.

I return to the car, but there's no sign of her; nobody else is around, the parking lot is emptying.

I go to the supermarket. The guard is still there, standing calmly, very calmly, obedient. Excuse me sir, the thing is that I'm looking for someone, I'm looking for someone this tall, with hair like this. I'm looking for her, how should I know where she went? She entered through the door there and that's the last thing I know for sure. The guard is nervous, he won't meet my eyes, fixes his on some blind spot to avoid looking at me. Can you please look me in the eyes, sir? This is important, she's nowhere to be found, I haven't seen her for hours. The guard puts a hand to his gun. Tell me the woman's name, otherwise I can't help you, he says. I don't want to answer, but hear words issuing from my mouth: A woman, a woman, a woman, again and again, as if it was the only thing I knew how to say. This is like a loop, a whirlpool, and once again that sensation of going around in circles and falling. What does the woman look like, what does the woman look like, what does the woman look like? the guard asks me, gripping his gun more tightly each time.

María? María, where are you? Hundreds of bodies and faces appear in my memory, creating a wall. Flesh, just flesh, piles of men on piles of women forming a mass that blocks off anything beyond it. Salvador, one of those bodies says as it rolls toward me, I heard you talking inside my belly and I was so frightened that I ran to tell a neighbor and she said: You should have kept it a secret, because now you'll have a normal child, like any other.

Sir, are you listening? If you don't tell me the name of the person you want to find and what she looks like, I can't help you, says the guard. Speak up, I can't hear. Sir? Her name. What's her name?

Why does he want to know her name? Why does he want to know my name? Damned fool, I say, but instead, what comes out of my mouth is a stream of vomit. Nausea is forcing my soul out with the food. Why is he asking me so many pointless questions? I bite off a sliver of nail and watch the blood appearing on my cuticle.

He's behind me now, I can hear the sound of his boots on the asphalt, even though they scarcely touch it. He'd made a move for his gun, I'm sure of that. The sound of his footsteps is louder. I don't turn, just go on running. Hundreds of eyes watching me, but I can't make out the individuals, can only see their eyeballs forming a single gaze. At the speed I'm travelling, everything merges into one shapeless mass of colors: wall, dog, tree, and person, oranges and flowers, dirty water swept by brooms, the brooms themselves, the fleeing rat. I believe that at some point I'm going to disappear, I ask my body to disappear, but it doesn't respond. My lungs slow me down, but something like a kind of parasite, a huge stream of vomit trying to get out of my guts, impels me forward. Then someone grabs my wrist and the energy my body had put into running has a recoil effect, the way a chained dog is tugged back by the force it put into getting free. I fall to the ground, there's red blood on my palms. A hand supports me and I have the marks of five very slender fingers on my arm, so well defined that a mold could be made from the indentations.

Why are you running, young man?

I'm getting up, but the man is still holding me, he removes his hand and I turn around. Huge relief. It isn't the guard but a storekeeper. The market has closed, behind the curtains and metal grills, I can make out herbs and other live plants. There's a pervasive smell of rotting fruit and, given the darkness, he must be the last trader to leave. His is the only light in the passage, but I'm not really sure what he sells. Are you okay? he asks. Yes, I say, a security guard was following me. Did you steal something? No, the guard was getting my goat or I was getting his goat, one of the two. I'm looking for a woman.

The red eyes of the desert wind turbines cast their glow over dust covering the city, I can see it through the leaves of the steel grill; the storekeeper tosses a coin into the air and the red light is reflected in that too.

The desert isn't far from here, right? I ask and the trader smiles. You'll need water and some fruit if you're going in there, he says. Then he rummages in the shadows and when he turns around to face me, he's holding out a bag. In the dim light I can see it contains a bottle of water and a few apples. Go along the road that's shining here in the streetlight, take a right at the first junction, it's a couple of hours' walk, and watch out for snakes.

We're all looking for a woman, he laughs, and I head off.

IV
The Other
of Oneself

Salvador drives in the center of the road without checking to see if anything else is coming in either direction; he takes it for granted that his is the only car in the desert and he may be right. Except for those vehicles of pure metal that make their way on enormous wheels over the mountains of earth, bringing sick people or sacks of salt and flour from other places, he's the only person driving something capable of moving at that speed over the rough terrain of a highway under construction. Even so, he has to brake; he brakes when two skinny dogs cross in front of him and the heat of the skid causes a tire to burst. Salvador has heard something hitting the hood of the car, a thud, like sacks of salt when they're being thrown into piles. He saw those two dogs crossing the highway and had to brake, there was nothing else for it. He's worried he may have killed one of them, because even though, as he gets out of the car, he tells himself not to be so dumb; because even though he thinks, Look at yourself, stopping for a couple of dogs that would have starved to death anyhow, Salvador is very frightened. He'd noticed the rhythm of the gait of those dogs as they were crossing and thought it couldn't be natural. They produced that sensation blue roses give when you look at them for too long: *Blue roses don't exist in nature*, but they still exist. As a child, he'd learned how to cut the stems and leave them soaking in paint for a few days until the petals turned blue and then, all too soon, the roses died. A decisive moment, like when sick people seem beautiful the day before their death.

Those dogs were walking in absolute unison, one lifting its leg at the exact same moment as the other, as though he were its shadow. A military escort of dogs, with the same sized bodies made of sheer blackness. Their eyes weren't visible, not even in the sunlight.

Salvador stands by the car door. He sees one of them stretched out, the body fused with the earth like a piece of black wax in the sun. It's blood, that's blood over there. The last time he'd seen dead blood, it was his mother's. His father, on the other hand . . . How had his father died? He can't remember for the moment. The dark patch in which the dog is emptying itself out has his whole attention: it slowly extends over the ground, through the dust, the smoke, the sun piercing everything, except that blood. The sun can't get in there. It must be thick, must be like the blood of the dog that used to guard his mother and, when it died, bled such a great volume of dark blood that his father said: My goodness, this is blacker than the Lord of Poison.

Absorbed in that memory, Salvador walks from his car toward the corpse. The other dog has disappeared; it may be hiding in the bushes, watching its shadow-brother die. Salvador moves a little closer, putting a hand over his nose as if there were already an awful stench, but what he finds doesn't have the form of an animal: it's a girl lying in her blood, a very young girl with her face fixed on the sky and her guts splattered on the earth.

There's a sweet smell in the air, a flowery smell, the smell of orange blossom.

The desert people, their legs dusty up to the calves even when they are sleeping, hear a car pass late at night. They hear a distant explosion. One of the women runs out with a loaded rifle to guard the three-street village. What was that? she calls to her neighbor, who replies from his window: Some damned lunatic drove through in a car, sister, must be one of those druggies who come here to feel all mystical. He must have had a blowout. Let's go back to sleep. After that, the whole village returns to bed. They have to be up very early in the morning. Before sunrise water has to be fetched from the well; before sunrise the water has to be taken to the mules and goats; feet are covered in dung. The women milk the goats and make two cheeses from the curds. One to sell, one to eat. There's no time to go to see who the madman is or to help him change the tire. They'll find out soon enough, because that's the way of things; you find out everything in these villages. Eventually those longed-for trivialities become great events; sometimes they pass from generation to generation as stories, so that fool who's driven into the desert could be making history. An occasional person turns up every few years and it seems like nobody is aware of it, yet they all know where he's been. But tomorrow's another day; for now the early morning chill is freezing the water in their basins and the animals are sleeping one atop the other, packs of foxes butcher stray hens, and snakes sleep with their eyes open. Time to sleep. Early tomorrow morning, before the sun comes up, everything has to be done.

There goes Señor Juan with his rod, the children would whisper, and they'd run to hide among the prickly plants to watch him pass. His name was legendary: Juan Barrera, the old people said, was the most reckless of men, but he lost his wife in the war and his soul has been in his boots since then. Juan Barrera, said the women, was a stud and sowed his seed all around the Sierra. Juan was a hired gun, an evil sorcerer, said the children, at night he turned into a black dog with red eyes, until another wizard came along, put his hands over those eyes and took away all Juan's powers, and since then Juan has been scared.

Juan Barrera, son of Vicente Barrera and the eternally unwed Cástula Sánchez, may her damned soul rest in peace, bears his paternal surname like a self-imposed punishment. At heart, he likes the rolling double *r* of the name, it reminds him of the sound of an engine, of things in the distant city to which he has never returned. He was only there for a few years, attending night school, working as a laborer, and carrying with him, like some form of Sisyphus, the moldy letters that were a reminder of who he was and what he'd done.

Juan slid into decline after losing his last hope. Something changed after Lázaro's death; his absence was like a knife turning inside him and it grew like a bad seed. Juan's grief was barely perceptible, it allowed him to keep on keeping on, to continue living and functioning. And as he was capable of action, he acted. Long shifts, three-hour nights, short naps on public transport. The mill. Double shifts at the mill and then a short nap, not long enough for dreaming, lying there on a bench. Night watchman or night school student. From those years, Juan only remembers the smell of poo coming from the children crawling between the desks while their mothers learned to read.

His grief was very deep rooted, like an illness you've gotten used to, or like a ghost that has manifested itself or that crouches inside while it feeds on you.

Later, new memories emerged, things he hadn't recalled for a long time: the day he and Lázaro found a rock with a fossil and realized that the desert had once been a sea; the families of coyotes that watched them from the undergrowth at night, the tapeta lucida behind their retinas shining like bright stars. In time, those memories had become clearer and he'd edited and ornamented some of his recollections, but there was always the seed lying beneath everything like a shadow.

In the classroom he'd been ashamed of his illiteracy; he'd heard the mocking laughter of the younger students, seen the bitter expressions of the pregnant women carrying children and notebooks in their arms. After so many hours of manual labor in the mornings and school at night, he'd finally come to know who he was. He would never have asked anyone else to read the letters to him: he knew that he alone must pull back the veil. He could never have borne the uninterested reading of a paid scrivener. He'd come a long way since the day he'd left the cave, but he was still furious; rage was an automatic response. The real war had finished long ago, but Juan had been trapped in another time. In his view, the fight was still going on. Sick of the world and, given the sacrifices needed to be a sociable man, he left the mill where he was working and decided to go back to the desert. He bought a few goats, got hold of a rifle, let his beard grow, and tied back his long, straggly, gray hair in a ponytail.

The rifle was there to discreetly show to other herders whenever one of their flock happened to escape and stray onto his dusty land. He never threatened anyone, but he'd pick up his gun and stare at the onlookers with those eyes like windows opening onto a wall. That was all it took, soon everyone knew it was better to keep on the right side of him.

In order to live that life, he needed to appear to be a legendary figure, to adopt a malevolent expression, create an aura of mystery. It wasn't hard: the pain of being who he was, the grief—still weightier than the now distant but still piercing pain of losing Lázaro—could only be endured by permanent rage. The fire of anger was his fuel, it passed through his skin, his bones, and made its presence felt.

Thirst is hunching him over. Thirst and dust, and the glaring sun that burns like the reflection from a mirror or a perfectly polished coin; all this makes him appear savage. He's been walking for too long. He calls out, trying to say a name, but for a few seconds even the coyotes think what they hear are howls and crouch among the dragon's blood trees. Is it a brother? they ask. Now, however, they can see the black dot that seems to be a man and quickly disperse, knowing that he's crying. How terrible the crying of men is for us, how terrible we feel to be near the shadows of men, only dogs can live with the wailing of men, not us, we can't bear it, they say to each other, and run for their dens.

Salvador walks on, unable to understand why he can no longer speak. Rage, thirst, a word, something is choking him. Just a few hours before he could still remember her name; it was a huge effort, but he could still say María. And he thought how dearly he loved her and wondered where she'd gotten to. And he remembered that when he first met her he said to himself: This woman is like a branch that never bends and, since it never bends, one day a strong wind will snap it.

He wanted to be that strong wind, wanted to test whether, despite everything she'd had to bear, she could still be broken. Such dignity, the jet-black hair falling around her face, so pretty when she cried.

A few hours before, Salvador had still known whom he was looking for, but since the episode at the supermarket certain ideas had been erecting walls against others, turning his mind into a large white room. It must be due to the sun beating down on his lids or because he now understood that he was truly without hope. His head had turned into a huge room full of nothing. He became aware that when—for all he tried to prevent it—his eyes turned inward and the pain of the nerves and muscles supporting his eyeballs caused the nausea to return. The pain was crippling, but around him there were only thorns to fall on. Salvador finally sank onto them, as slowly as a fighter who doesn't realize he's wounded until he pauses to rest.

Juan is sleeping. His body is stretched out beside the sheet he's kicked off and his jawbone creaks because even when asleep he grinds his teeth. He clenches his jaw the way dogs do when they've managed to get hold of a piece of meat and won't let go. Juan, his mouth full of invisible meat, is sleeping. He dreams that an enormous shadow, not the usual darkness of night, has appeared to fill the whole room, and is watching him. He keeps his eyes closed so as to avoid the confirmation that there, in and outside his dream, he really is being watched by a dense, darkening mass. A few moments before, tenuous moonlight was falling on the table, but then everything turned to nothing. Juan has no idea how that watchful monster can move the vast darkness of its body so effortlessly. Fear; the night is suddenly heavy, tomorrow he'll find the cats dead, their fur damp, as if an enormous monster had smothered them in its mouth.

Opening his eyes is as hard as making a cut in flesh to suck out poison. At that hour of the night, darkness has massed in his desert room and its gaze is a lash. Who's looking at him this way? Who's holding his gaze, even through the thin layer of flesh covering his eyes?

Juan eventually opens his eyes and has the sense that they had never in fact had lids. Peeled eyes, half-open in the night that has taken up residence in the room. Everything here is filled by the dark being that observes him with its small, yellow eyes. The glasses, the plates, the pots standing on the embers, everything has been filled to overflowing with blackness. He's certain of that. When the thing looks at him, he immediately remembers his mother, her two breasts uncovered to feed him with the alcohol of her milk, two black, very black lumps that were his only view when she sat him on her lap and sang him a sad, drunkard's song. He isn't sure if he's still dreaming or is awake, but he does know that the thing is staring at him, and its gaze is so heavy he can't close his eyes. Who are you? he asks, but when he speaks all the air disappears from his mouth. He's left dry, dry. There isn't a drop of blood in his body, no air in his lungs. It feels as if the thing has filled him too, that he's completely full of whatever it is; the shadow has gotten in through his eyes.

Lázaro, is that you?

Lázaro, have you come to demand something more of me? Because I want to tell you that I did all I could. I even killed his wife, Lázaro, to take our revenge. I went to his house and saw her sitting under an orange tree, wearing a pale-colored dress, peeling fruit with her teeth. Our father's wife was so pretty, Lázaro, so young and fresh. That fucking old man, his wife was like a dark-skinned saint sitting under her tree, her eyes fixed on that white pith of the fruit. Can I help you, son? she said. Are you Vicente Barrera's wife? In a soft, trembling voice, she told me that she was. And then, Lázaro, I had a clear memory of Vicente, our father, and my fingers closed on the knife and when I attacked her and felt her blood flowing down my hand, a dog appeared from nowhere and bit my hands until I managed to kill them both. The dog's blood was thick, but hers gushed out like water. I took our revenge, Lázaro. Our father would die without that woman. That's hitting where it really hurts, an eye for an eye, a tooth for a tooth.

Juan speaks to the blackness: Lazarito, I'm always talking to you, but it's years since you've replied. I didn't talk to you when I should have done and look where that silence got us: you're dead and I'm still a soldier, even though the war really is over now.

Juan is in that place where the rage of a warrior goes when it's no longer needed. He came here because it's a place where nobody can harm him and so far from everything that he can't harm anyone else. It was true that someone had been stalking them, true they were fleeing from something awful, something disgusting, but the thing that hounded them was within themselves and couldn't be removed: it circulated, pulsed, coated their hearts. Juan can still hear that strange passenger when he's silent and no sounds can be heard in the valley. Sometimes there is so little noise that he can hear the workings of his own body, the machine that circulates the blood of his enemy.

When Lázaro died, Juan made him a promise: to take revenge on their father. And when he finally read the letters, he set out in search of him. In those nocturnal whisperings, he wasn't going to recount the memory, tell Lázaro's ghost about the years of anguish in the school, the mockery, the derision, the awful weariness, the dead years. When, through the photos, Juan discovered that they shared a father, when he recalled his mother, his soul left his body. He's still in this world, but is the shell of a man with no inner man. A specter, a doleful mark in time, is all that is left of the soldier Lázaro loved. His sorrow has made him a specter, and he will remain here in torment even after his death.

Lázaro, he says, Lazarito, but you've already met your death and it was just in time, before you discovered all that.

When Lázaro found him, his father was a dog, a wild animal; so he turned his back and forgot. It's often the case that the best thing you can do is nothing.

Look at this miserable specimen, Lázaro, says Juan, show yourself, say something to me.

And he lies there whimpering until sleep overcomes him, but he's scarcely nodded off when he again senses the darkness stalking him as if it were his death; he quickly opens his eyes and in them can be seen the reflection of his fleeting dream where blood pulses loudly.

Juan believes he remembers all the people he's killed, but that blood is his own blood, the blood of Vicente Barrera, the itinerant seller of yarns, and of the eternally unwed Cástula Sánchez, who was born a woman with a big heart and died with an enlarged liver. You can't choose your family. When Juan was a baby, he'd cling to his mother's breast as if he were going to die, he bit on her nipples with his gums and his mother would pinch his tiny legs. She left bruises. And some days, when Juan's bare legs hung outside her rebozo, teeth marks were visible. As a small boy, he slept all day due to the alcohol in her milk or the aguardiente she dripped from her little finger into his mouth.

You die many times during a life, Lazarito, thinks Juan, still in conversation with his own dead, although not like you— you really upped sticks and left me—not like Cástula; though she was flesh and blood, she was already fully dead when I was born. And despite the fact that Juan is arguing with a shade, he suddenly becomes aware of loud noises outside. He's so filled with guilt that it's never easy for him to tell whether what he hears are laments or the wind blowing the sand.

One night merged into another, unifying time and the blackness. Juan lay restless on his mattress on the floor, thinking ants were crawling up his legs so, late as it was, he got up to find them and burn them alive. He heard the whimpers coming from outside; they seemed closer and then the whole valley went quiet. The coyotes weren't howling, there were no owls hooting, from time to time the air moved in imitation of a woman's voice and Juan was frightened; he clenched his fists and went to fetch his rifle. It was three in the morning, the time that in the village they called "the hour of the spirits." When he left the house, guided by a small lamp, he went to the edge of his plot but saw nothing. He was too scared to light up the darkness and the night was moonless. In the pitch black, only his body was haloed by the lamp.

He was alone, yet could still hear the cries of the previous night, a hoarse voice.

I don't recognize that animal, he said in alarm, and walked quickly back to his house.

And the same happened the next day, this time under the fiery sun that produced a grand spectacle of red skies in the evenings. Juan heard the voice again and fear made his facial muscles twitch as if hot pepper had been rubbed into them. He ran out of the house, carrying the loaded rifle, ready to shoot someone. He walked his land, walked beyond it, went as far as the small group of withered trees that hid things in their shadows and found insects, stones, and finally, the man. He was some way from the house, lying face down behind a dry yucca. It seemed clear that he'd gotten lost, you could see it in his shoes—dirty, but in good condition—and pants, which had none of the holes the corrosive desert dust eventually makes, but were partially covered in thorns and crusts of sand. He'd been lying there for a long time.

He's not from these parts, said Juan. He moved the man's head: the lips were parted, his eyes closed, but he was mumbling something. Well, he was alive, but how many nights had he been there, whimpering, not far from the house, scaring him? He definitely isn't from these parts; any local would have known how to orientate himself by the mountain that from a distance looks like a resting tiger, but he'd gotten lost in the maze of a stretch of flat ground that goes on and on with more of the same for miles. This desert is a trickster. You tell yourself that palm tree is different from the one before, but it's the same palm. You can go around in circles for days here, believing you're getting somewhere. And that's why the desert is only for the people who live in it. You have to walk here for a long time before being able to tell the difference between one branch and another, one rock and another, one cactus and another; when you really look, the paths become clear.

Juan knew the desert, knew it was the best place to find refuge, the place that used to confuse enemies during the war. What the sea was for mariners, the desert was for soldiers: full of unimaginable monsters, hellish creatures, stories about God and the Devil, and hostile plants that burn and cause children to develop fevers. If you're lucky, there are also kindly cacti that offer bitter nopals, even though water never reaches their roots.

But this man must be stupid to come in here without knowing the place, thought Juan. And that's why, Lázaro, it was good that you died when you did, because otherwise you'd have had to see the face of this fool I've found in the shadows; his skin is burned, the chill evening wind has burned him as much as the sun.

Juan asked him his name again and again.

Half-dead, the man replied that he was called María.

That's right, the man said his name was María.

The man says his name is María and Juan thinks of Lázaro, of his curves and how sometimes being with him was like being with a woman. To be honest, they look alike; there's a resemblance between that man and Lázaro.

He's carrying a jar, cradling it, and doesn't even let go when Juan turns him over, searches his pockets, and in the small one over his heart discovers his name: Salvador. On his ID—the ID of a morgue employee—the face is clean-shaven. This man has my father's surname, thinks Juan. The thought of Vicente always makes him light-headed, sets his body awash with blood straight from the liver, clenches his fists, disheartens him. Then, without warning, the man speaks, the man wakes and in a feminine voice says: My father bit my legs and dumped me in the trash, covered in bruises; my mother had to give me a good slap to make me breathe again.

Juan gazes at him for a while and ideas coalesce in his mind, forming a leaden mass: huge confusion. And that confusion makes the old soldier furious, something inside him is feeding his fury, causing the automatic reaction of a kick to Salvador's ribs. Salvador lets out a long, frightful arrgh and then falls silent.

Juan walks away, goes about his business, and as he feeds the hens, he murmurs: Salvador Barrera thinks he's a woman, just like you, Lázaro; his voice goes all soft when he says his name is María and even softer when, as María, he says Salvador. He doesn't understand that everything about him is male and that he's the man he's talking about.

It's a long time since Juan had the sense of something new, like when he was a child and the priests brought toys for their favorites. He dashes out of the house like a small boy, goes back to Salvador's inert body, turns it a little, wakes him, helps him to sit up.

Can you tell me where you've come from?

With a strange expression in his eyes, barely able to sit upright, Salvador says: I've come from the city, I'm lost. Salvador cheated on me with another woman and I'm lost. Haven't you ever been in love? It's so hard to think of someone you love loving someone else, but I saw them together, I really saw them, naked. He was fucking her like she was the only person he'd ever done it with. I don't know what happened next, I'm here and I'm thirsty.

As Juan looks on, the man speaks and then passes out, speaks and then passes out again, he looked as though he were drunk, or drugged, or possessed. Juan decides to carry him into the house, but the man resists, saying: You want to rape me, but if Salvador finds me first, he'll kill you. The man screams as he's dragged along. Juan puts a hand over his mouth and says: Be quiet or I'll kill you. And he pushes him into the room where the night before something had looked into his eyes through his closed lids.

Walking in his sleep, Salvador goes to the fire the way a child approaches a mock crucifixion. He's dreaming that María's hair is flying around her face, blown by the current of air entering through the car's sunroof; she looks like a drawing of a jellyfish, he thinks. She interrupts the long silence to tell the same story one more time:

Have you ever seen the stiffness leave a corpse after you've spoken to it, Salvador? I once watched a woman dressing her son, she couldn't get his shirt on because of the rigor and, firm as a tree, the mother said to him: Surrender, child, just surrender, it's God's will, and better to surrender to death, this is the only time worth admitting you're beaten; if you die so angry, you'll have nightmares, so let me put your shirt on; hey, my boy, you'll look so handsome. And with tears running down her face, the woman was finally able to bend his arms and it even looked as though the boy himself were putting on the shirt.

Why are you telling me that story again? he replies without turning to look at her. Since the journey had begun, he's avoided meeting her eyes, pretending to be focused on driving well, but even during the stops at tollbooths he's looked the other way.

It isn't actually the same story. Didn't you notice that I've changed some of the details? Does it bother you that I'm telling it again?

No, it doesn't bother me, I'm just wondering what that story has to do with us now, he thinks, but doesn't reply.

What's in the jar, Salvador?

My father's remains.

María looks shocked.

Why do you still hang on to him?

I don't know, María. He's my father.

Yes, but your father was mad, Salvador. He bit your legs so hard that your screams almost choked you and he used to hit your mother.

Where did you get that idea? My father was a good man.

Have you already forgotten? That's the problem with death: it dignifies people. Have you forgotten that your father was a savage beast? He had to be kept under lock and key so he wouldn't escape. He used to launch himself at women to bite them, he walked on all fours, and he was killed when his chain strangled him or broke his neck. Do you really not remember, Salvador?

Shut up, María. I don't know why you say such things, I honestly don't know where you got all that stuff from, you're mixing things up. I had a good father, an old but educated person, a good man. Don't laugh that way, stop laughing, María. You scare me when you laugh that way.

What did your father die of, Salvador?

I can't remember right now.

What do you mean, you can't remember right now? Who forgets how their father died? You're such an idiot.

I won't have you talking to me like that, stop laughing. For the love of God, María, it frightens me when you laugh that way, stop this minute . . .

The deafening laughter wakes Juan, who opens his eyes at

the exact moment Salvador, with his eyes closed, puts his hand in the fire. He runs toward Salvador, but doesn't try to stop him, simply watches, watches as that sleeping madman, killing himself laughing, puts his hand in the fire and serenely inhales the scent of charring flesh.

The night weighs heavy. In the past, in the present, in the future, everywhere, on days like these the night grows heavy. The true blackness comes calling. And poor Juan, speaking alone, says: Lázaro, tell me something, you're dead and so know everything, send me a sign, show me the right path. See how I speak to you as though you were God, for pity's sake, help me. What's that man doing with his jar? I tried to open it last night, but it's sealed. He won't be parted from it. I've thought that it might contain gold, I've thought the man has come to the desert looking for what they all want to find here: gold. What should I do? He bears our surname. The one I too use to remind myself that I'm damned, because I couldn't save you from death and then I killed our father's wife. And because I used to fuck you, Lázaro, and we were brothers. I can't go on living with the memory of all that, don't you see? That's why I think I'm going to kill him too. I don't know what to do. I honestly don't know. This morning, I tied him up, because he's getting to look more and more like a wild dog. Last night, he howled until dawn before finally falling asleep. And he says his name is María and also that he's called Salvador, and Salvador says he's looking for María and María says she's looking for Salvador. I don't understand the first thing. I can't bear it anymore, I'm going to kill him, Lázaro. Anyway, now the Devil has me in his clutches, one more death makes no difference, it'd be good to have that feeling again, the feeling you get when you know someone is dying and just for a moment everything in the world pales by comparison. You feel as light as a ghost. So, so light. That's why I want to kill him too, and maybe then he'll stop barking and let me sleep. And what if he is our brother? How many others can possibly share our damned blood?

Poor Juan, lost in his monologue, burning with fever or emotion, or the heat that comes from holding back tears, calls out to Lázaro, the person who rotted away in a cave, covered by a blanket, he calls out to Lázaro, his sturdy lover, the lover who rotted alone while the cave filled with birds.

I'm glad you died when you did, Lazarito, so you didn't have to see this. By the third day, the man who says his name is María resembled a rabid dog. He spat, barked, howled, launched himself at me, biting, and I was forced to tie him up to a tree. I guess everyone saw me and I felt as though something huge and dark was watching me through their eyes. And my dearest Lazarito, even the trees had eyes, says Juan, kneeling before an improvised cross he's made by nailing two logs together.

Possibly he thought he'd been seen by the children who came to his land looking for a good place to take a shit. They were always spying on him, but this time they saw what they had been hoping to see; something out of the ordinary. Tied to the trunk of the tree in the yard was a man who looked wild, savage. His eyes were horrible, bloodshot eyes. Come on, let's see what's going on, said the children, moving a little closer. But no, they weren't human eyes, they were the eyes of a dead man; but even so, the pupils moved and projected their infinite emptiness onto wherever they were directed. The children scented danger and left. It was three days before they opened their mouths again. Their grandmas had to spit alcohol on their shoulders, bathe them in flowers, make them chew on the skins of snakes.

Salvador's body was there, but he himself had gone. In his mind, he'd continued on his way into the desert. He could hear the distant crying of the coyotes and was surprised to see that, even in winter, the sun went down at such a speed that it looked like a shooting star. When he was silent, he sometimes heard María's voice. He'd be chasing the shadow of a cactus and suddenly notice that when the sun set so quickly, those shadows seemed to come alive. And the shadows of the yuccas were shaped like a woman.

Salvador rested on a rock from time to time, he was walking without feeling thirst, without wondering when he was going to eat or if he was even hungry. The calm warmed his stomach, like when he lay on María and one of them then the other would breathe, and then, almost automatically, their breathing would fall into the same rhythm and it was no longer possible to tell who the sound of the air going in and out belonged to. They would sleep like that or lie awake, but with a sense of deep repose. In that state, chasing cactus shadows seemed fun. María, he'd call. María, don't hide! As if the whole thing were a game. María, come out, he'd call, running behind some plant only to discover there was nobody there. And at night, without him knowing exactly how, the simplest fire he made had never been prepared by his own hands, and he'd drop dry yucca in there to hear it crackle strangely in the flames, and like María's body when he lay on her and their bones fitted in together, or the mattress creaking and the wooden headboard banging against the wall in a drumbeat that set their blood racing and had her moaning like a coyote cub. And the birds also flew around with great ease, as though they had always been gliding on the wind; Salvador would fall asleep in front of his simple fire and wait for another day to begin so he could search for María.

Those moments of calm, however, would be interrupted by long fights with someone who was almost formless. Something that kicked him in the ribs, dragged him around, covered his mouth, stood over him to administer punishment. And he'd react—what else could he do if he wanted to finally find María? The fights were awful, both inside himself and outside. Salvador's eyes might be vacant, but he could still make out each and every scratch. He never missed one, like a wild animal protecting its young.

All those fights took place because Juan would wake from bad dreams in which he again felt he was being watched by a dark mass, a blood that enveloped him like clouds when they loom low and the air becomes so dense that a man in mid duel couldn't see his opponent. The sky in the dream was black: it was disgusting, nauseating. And for nothing more than that sensation, that anguish when he woke, Juan made the decision to kill the wild man.

His plan was to dig a grave to bury him in after the death, but when he started on the task, the earth refused to open up. He put all his strength behind the spade, but nothing happened. He walked for yards, trying to make his hole, but the earth seemed to have become hard as a diamond. While he was wielding the mattock, while he was grubbing with his fingers in the unyielding ground, he heard giggles and the earth still refused to open up. Time after time, it wouldn't open up. Give me a break! he cried. Either you go home or you'll feel this mattock in your faces too! He thought it was the children, but there was no response, not even from the few dry leaves or the rough stones that crumble when you tread on them. He scoured the whole of his land, scratching the ground, trying to force in the spade, the mattock, but there was no possibility of digging a hole. The earth was firm set, while he was like a dog rolling in the dirt. What the hell's going on? I'm not crazy, said Juan, sitting on a rock and starting to talk to Lázaro again.

Lázaro, have you come to visit me? Last night, I dreamed of the darkness again, and then that you were walking in the desert, dying of hunger, and you came across a wounded dog. You killed it with a rock and started to eat the meat, but it had rotted very quickly and the wormy flesh was falling apart in your hands. Here, try some, Juan, you said, and I opened my mouth for your foul-smelling flesh, like when I used to receive the host from the priests.

The next day the dawn orchestra woke everyone. It was the cry of an animal in heat, a large animal, howling pitifully, withdrawing into itself and howling again. Juan ran outside to silence the beast; he untied it so he could flog it more easily. He no longer called the animal by its names—Salvador, María; by then he was treating it like a dog, kicking its snout when it walked on all fours. So he untied it without taking into account that it was now stronger, without taking into account that it might bite him, clench its jaws and drag him around the yard, so the rocks and thorns would further damage the tough skin of his back, already marked by the scars of knife and bullet wounds; a real war painting. Juan fought back, but the beast was too much for him; despite the blows that had already fallen on its body, it dragged him around as best it could and then withdrew into itself again to continue howling. Howling in the light of day. Juan got to his feet, covered in dirt, and heard laughter. The children again, he thought. He went for his rifle and shot a few bullets into the air, but the laughter continued. The animal, on the other hand, had taken refuge by the tree where it had been tied up, so it was easier for Juan to grab the cords and tether it again. They were both oozing reddish blood: in Juan's case, seeping through the material of his pants and shirt; in the beast's, soaking the fur on its head.

Juan didn't sleep that night either. He felt once again that he was being watched, once again had the sense that something was holding his gaze through his closed eyelids. The following day, before opening the drapes, he reached out for his gun and went into the yard toward the savage. It was repeating María over and over. Occasionally it stopped, dozed, and when it woke repeated Salvador, Salvador, Salvador.

I've had it up to here, you lunatic, Juan said, and fired his gun until he ran out of ammunition.

Juan's aim wasn't true or none of the bullets hit their mark. Maybe the dog had merged with the soil in his plot of land, maybe everything, including his beast, was filled with blackness, and so impenetrable.

What's going on? he wondered, thinking for a moment of his ageing body. He'd been the best sharpshooter in his squadron and now he couldn't make a single hit. The wretched dog was at the far end of the yard, withdrawn into itself, trembling.

I've had enough of you, you damned loco, said Juan, pressing the trigger again even though he knew he was out of ammo. He fetched the jar and, not really knowing what to do with it, in a fit of fury dashed it against a rock, but instead of gold, it was ashes that flew out. A dust cloud formed; the wind blew through and lifted Vicente's ashes into the air, covering Juan's corneas with the gray particles that didn't smell anything like the way the dead smell. Juan beat his fists on the ground. Who'd have thought a dead person could burn your eyes that way? He didn't understand the first thing. Why was that crazy imbecile carrying a load of dust around with him? He should have known. Right from the start he'd seen that the man was insane, so how could he have put so much faith in finding something valuable in the jar? Foolishness, he said, and again went for Salvador, who was lying on the ground with his eyes closed. On your feet, you animal, on your feet. The dog, the savage, didn't obey. It had pissed itself and its body was rigid with fear. Then it opened its lids and looked into Juan's eyes. And, for an instant, Juan reexperienced that sensation he used to have when he looked at Lázaro: communion, tenderness swelling inside him.

Enough is enough, he said, I can't bear any more. And he sat down on his tree trunk, took a stick, and doodled in the sand; the shape was probably a flower or maybe a knot.

At break of day, he threw a few pails of water over the savage. It stood on all fours, trembling, then ran scared toward a sunnier spot and rolled in the dirt until it felt less naked. We'll have to change your name, said Juan, more to himself than to the dog. I'm going to call you Snubnose, and if you behave yourself, I'll call you Pigface. Juan laughed, laughed hard, his laughter careened around in his guts, causing him to laugh even harder. Salvador, the savage, was lying in the sun getting a golden tan, his thoughts miles away. In his mind, he was walking through the desert, his clothing clean and pressed, searching for María. He looked for her under the yuccas, among the magueys. Wild horses ran past him, raising a dust storm that mingled with the mist that hung around the rock faces in the mornings. María! And an echo answered him in a woman's voice: María! The voice came and went with the same name following behind, ringing loud as if the high plain were completely empty; no plants, no venomous animals, no wild horses, no trees, no him. He walked for hours that night, unsurprised that he wasn't carrying a flashlight or lantern; he could see perfectly in the dark and at times had the feeling he was following the trail of some wounded or rutting animal.

Also that night, while he was walking through that high plain—a high plain that seemed to have changed color, form, everything—his nose scented a female and, without the first idea how, he appeared there, in the squadron of males running behind the bitch. She twirled like a whirlwind, then ran at full tilt, limping on one foot and then another due to the thorns of those button cacti that coyotes remove by pressing themselves against rocks, at risk of driving them further in; they never use their snouts because the thorny buttons get on their lips so they can't eat, or swallow, or whimper with the pain that rekindles fire or makes it dance.

Salvador joined the line behind the female, not really certain if it was a woman, a bitch, a nanny goat, or the memory of somebody who had turned into something else. Every part of him was focused on the cleft, on finding a hole to put all his lust into. And the bitch, or woman, or nanny goat—or maybe it was even a yucca that was running there—howled because it had had enough of pups, or children, or seeds, and behind her went the male dogs, unperturbed, blind to everything around them, but with the genital eye dribbling, throwing out flames and a smell that filled the air like smoke.

Salvador woke with his penis in a tree. Something weird is going on here, he told himself.

María?

He repeated and chanted the name over and over until his intonation became so mechanical it lost all meaning: far off, what the coyotes heard wasn't a name, just barks.

Grandma, said the little one, Señor Juan has a bald dog. Juan Barrera has gotten a dog? The women didn't believe he was capable of loving and caring for anything. Even his goats wandered around lost and blind. He sometimes milked them, but mostly the poor things were left with their udders bursting and bleeding. A hairless dog, son? Are you sure? Yes, Grandma, it looks like a man. And the ladies, who never let the grass grow under their feet, got together immediately and drank aguardiente, being careful to hold a little back in their mouths to spit on the children's backs. They stuck certain flowers on their eyelids with nopal juice. God bless your souls, you're imagining things, they said. Don't hang around his place anymore, children, there's something not right about that man. But the children insisted: First we thought it was a man or a lady, but it's a dog. Is it catching, Grandma? 'Cause I feel kind of crazy, I want to run out of here and lasso a horse, or tear a hen apart with my teeth. The women drank, the women laughed together, and whispered, and their murmuring lulled the children to sleep. Then the women crossed themselves time and again before leaving, and said: God bless you, God be with you. And some whistled tunes as they walked home.

One of them went to her husband in the night, lowered his pants, and in a whiney voice said: Tell me something, husband. The girls are all in the next room, wouldn't you like to burn them? That was all she said, but everything was so quiet that her voice carried to the other room and when the girls heard her words, they fled.

A question, some coyotes, the light footsteps of the runaways.

After that, the desert returned to silence.

The octopus that dreams of being a stone turns into
one; the desert was once a sea, and that's perhaps why the animals here do the same: cold-blooded scorpions and some other
bugs that camouflage themselves when they are sleeping turn
into what they dream too, which is why people passing through
sometimes see sleeping women, or they see eyeless fish swimming in the waters of the air. It's the land giving those working
on it the signal to rest, the signal that the sun is wreaking havoc,
water is running short, that they've ingested too much of the
plant that makes you want to walk or maybe peyote bruto. Then
the muleteers and the women rest in the shade or, if there is
none, in the sun; they sleep sitting or standing and after a while
they return to their tasks. They walk to the village and everyone
is in the church at that hour. The church, or perhaps it would
be better to say the ugly shack where they all hang their crosses.
The only place other than the women's altars where there are
fresh flowers every day and the scent of death and tuberoses.
Inside, someone comments in a hushed tone that Señor Juan
has a hairless dog, that gunshots have been heard, that the look
in the dog's diabolical eyes left the young'uns struck dumb for
days. We had to feed them snake meat for the poison, says one
old lady. Poison, Doña Ligia? Why poison? Well, the children
say that when they looked the dog in the eyes, they thought
it was a man or a woman and the confusion made their heads

hurt like a poison, they had to lie down, some of them even came out in a rash, and others had fever. A dog that stings with its eyes, heavens above, says a man not far off. Damned venom.

The girls have come back, says Doña Ligia, but two of them aren't virgins now. Poor souls, replies another woman not far away. And they were wounded because at night a dog that looked like a man jumped out at them, they say it was chasing after the horses and if they hadn't run home, they were sure the dog would have eaten them; and it was a hairless dog, Señora Roselia, like the young'uns say. The murmuring mingles with the prayers. White noise, the sound of voices, each saying something different, the sound of them all standing after kneeling on the ground and then the slap of palms coming together. They give the sign of peace, kiss each other's foreheads, and agree to meet later to go visit Señor Juan and see the dog.

Juan was staring into space when the dog appeared in the doorway. The crusts of earth made it look as though it had a fine coat of fur. Pigface, you've come back, Juan said. And he swallowed his vexation and went over to the dog, which had, without warning, fallen asleep.

The dog was deep in its dreams; the dream of eyes half-open. Through the whites of those eyes entered a little of the real night, but in its dream it was daytime; a day with a very unusual sun whose light was red rather than orange. The mountains were reddish too and there were no birds. Salvador was calling: María! And the coyotes answered him. He didn't tire and neither was he surprised to find himself unharmed; at times he came across other humans, or birds, or dogs, and they hunted together, and sometimes he also made love with some woman and, while she was nibbling his ear, the stars would fall down to earth. Salvador, who is María? I don't know, he answered, I think that's just the way my bark sounds. And once again Salvador didn't understand why he'd said that, the transit through the inconstant spiral was broken, the delirium shattered, and Salvador woke from that dream with the realization that he was a man lost in the desert, looking at another man. And the other man was Juan, whose eyes were brimming with tears that night.

The trader's been here, Snubnose, and I said to myself: I don't believe it, not again, he's here and he hasn't changed one bit over all these years, I don't believe it; not a single wrinkle, he's just more deeply tanned, and that makes it look like a dark veil is stretched over his face. Damned scary. Fucking scary, I told myself and, without meaning to, I let out the first guffaw and I laughed so hard I thought I'd die. How on earth can it be true, Snubnose?

Juan started at the sound of his own voice and, in spite of his fear, tried to move closer to the dog. Lying in a narrow strip of shade, lost in its thoughts, the dog did and didn't hear him. Whenever it sensed Juan coming too close, it growled. It had returned with skin darkened by the sun and in that blackness only its teeth gleamed.

Juan said that when he saw the trader, he'd started to laugh and hadn't been able to stop. His laughter was as potent as infected saliva and went on and on like a persistent cough, loosening up his whole body until he finally fell to the ground and his cackling was like a viper that had spewed out of his mouth and was wrapping his body in a cool, smooth skin.

You've wet yourself, kid, said the trader, squatting down next to him. I was passing through these parts when I heard talk of a man who had a hairless dog that had raped some girls, although they'd later managed to escape. They wouldn't be talking about you, would they, Juan? So, where's the dog? Can I see it?

Juan's laughter bounced off the walls, his face was turning purple, his piss was getting darker and beginning to stink. With a grand flourish, the trader slapped his face. They're coming for you, he said. It's time to leave!

To prevent himself choking on his own laughter, Juan was forced to start crying. I've no idea where the dog is, he managed to say, it bit through the rope last night and ran off. It hasn't come back.

Look, Juan. I'm just going to tell you something. Please, no, replied Juan. No more stories. But the trader had already filled his lungs with air and started his tale:

As you know, my boy, the villagers get together at this hour to watch the sunset. Well, I passed through there yesterday and a woman was saying this: I finally recognized my hands, I stood there looking at them and said, These are what provide me with food, the part of me that best reflects my age, and I've never taken notice of them. I wanted to do some good for them and so I made an ointment with a little milk. See how smooth they are now. Go on, touch them. And the young girls sat around the woman and allowed her to braid their hair. For a long time, nobody spoke. It seemed like they all knew everything about everybody. How are your daughters doing, Ligia? one man asked. Better, but I won't be able to marry them off now. They'll have to go to work on the streets in the town. Who'll want them here the way they are? All knocked about. There was another silence and then suddenly Señora Ligia shrieked, it's dreadful, dreadful, and broke down in tears, loudly confessing that her girls were pregnant.

Pregnant by the dog? someone over there asked. God alone knows what sort of monster will come of it.

Did you give them the bitter herb?

Have you tried hawthorn, Ligia?

That's a sin and you know it as well as I do. Didn't we promise we'd never do it again? No, my girls will be proud to have their puppies.

But, Ligia . . .

But nothing, I've said my piece: they'll have their puppies.

The trader finished off by saying: So, you've been warned. A pleasure to meet you again, Juan! Congratulations on the growing family, he called from a distance, raising his hat. And off he went, toying with a coin, and tossing it high into the air, where it shone like a second sun, like the edge of a knife.

Juan had no chance to ask questions, when he came around from his fit of laughter, the dog was there: tanned, covered in crusts of dirt, dreaming in its eyes-half-open sleep. He put on its chain to take it to the backcountry, along with a mule and a cart loaded with water and blankets. We're leaving, he said. They're coming to kill us and I've no intention of dying at the hands of men, Pigface, much less when they're throwing stones. We're off. And the dog, which was very tired from hunting or believing it was fucking, followed Juan tamely.

The desert was becoming a different place. The whiteness of the ground in the moonlight made Juan think that if he dug a finger in it, milk would well up. The savage trotted along docilely on its chain. There's no more rope for you, Snubnose, you've been very bad, he said. The cold came on as soon as night fell, but they tried to get as far as possible from the village because otherwise a fire would be visible. Juan was certain they would come for them, would hunt them down, would kill his dog and kill him, tying his feet to the hooves of a sorrel horse in heat and mad with hunger. Or they'd stone him, or tie him to a yucca and burn him alive, the way they did with deserters. Only God and the Devil know how yucca smells when you set it afire near flesh, and how the holes in xoconostle cacti light up when filled with flames, he was thinking. So many hellish scenes here; blood doesn't quench the desert thirst and the coyotes howl, or laugh, or whatever they do, there's always a laugh now, or I can't remember life without laughter in the background, never silence, or maybe for me silence is deep laughter. I'll be damned if God isn't laughing at me. Such fear, such fear, he crooned again. Juan sat down by a rock and the savage lay beside him. If only you had fur, he said, but when he moved closer to cover himself a little with the hairless animal, the beast growled. Darned animal, moaned Juan. He unlaced his boots and, checking there were no scorpions around, rubbed the fine white powder lying over the earth on his feet. The scent of stagnant water, of dried blood and damp earth were carried to the dog, the man, and the insects, although the latter didn't even notice. The scent, nevertheless, pierced Juan like an ill omen. Time to start walking again, he ordered, tugging on the dog's chain, and the weary dog allowed itself to be pulled along.

He didn't know if they were buttocks or breasts, just inserted himself between those two mounds with something approaching cynicism, and then the bitch (or the nanny goat, or the yucca, or the shadow of the yucca) curled up and whimpered. And he realized that in place of a mouth, she had a flower that was vaguely like her sexual organs, and in place of an armpit, two rows of teeth that opened to release a woman's voice saying: Why do you treat me that way? Then the lower row moved lethargically upward and his penis was trapped. And so he spent hours, days, in the middle of the desert, copulating with the snout of a strange animal (or it may have been the body of a nanny goat, or the hollow of a tree, or just the chaotic memory of someone). But his dream was always shattered by the man who called himself his master and they would start walking together once more until the sun went down and, much against his will, Salvador would have the same dream. Days and weeks passed in that way, until Juan finally said: I think I can still see torches, but I'm weary, I refuse to walk any further.

The double life of the savage was hard, there were moments of lucidity when he returned and realized that he was a man who was down on his luck. Work, the rent, his car, that woman who looked into his eyes and said: You're a good man. All that lined up with the guard and the man in the market with a bag of apples to be inspected by his tired brain. And María? Where's María? So lovely when she cried, she gave the impression of being as desirable as the hollow of a tree, beautiful as a sturdy branch that, since it doesn't bend, would one day be blown to pieces by the wind. María, if I were ever to be born as a woman, I'd take your name, says Salvador, but Juan only hears him howling and so jokingly makes a swipe at him with a cloth. Be quiet, Snubnose, he says, they'll see us, but the dog curls up in a ball and blinks, expecting a real blow. Juan looks back into the distance.

I've seen children with torches coming this way, you can't make them out clearly because of the glare of the sun, but they're nearly here, and when they arrive they'll kill you and then they'll burn me alive.

Salvador no longer hears him; he's lost his wits again and is falling down a long slide that leads to his savage dream.

He was licking the citrus zone of a woman, or a shadow, or the memory of someone who has become something else: a yucca, a bitch, a hollow made with the hand, a hollow in a kindly fruit. The memory of someone who stings him while he's putting his penis in and—like his whole being—that piece of flesh in some way resembles a saguaro cactus standing erect despite the lack of water. Coming and going, with tears in his eyes, Salvador doesn't know against whom he's copulating. A spiral, a spiral opens up when he attempts to see her face, when he attempts to distinguish whether they are barks or bullets, or the voice of someone saying I love you. And from time to time he also has the sensation that he's introducing himself into a face, supported by thick lips, the lips of some unknown animal. Sometimes, when he's wholly Salvador—a state he's rarely in and that is of increasingly short duration—even while he's copulating, he remembers his mother, whose image, when it comes, is clear in his memory. She tells him: Child, your father used to say he once saw a woman in the mist; when he was selling yarns, your father saw many things, but he said that woman made such a particularly strong impression on him that he followed her for some yards, calling out to her; he said her head was lowered and she was sobbing, and that the mist seemed to be following her. And then, when he was almost beside himself, and I have to tell you this, Salvador: your father was a womanizer, and when he was fired up about some girl, there was no peace for her, as happened to me, but that doesn't matter now, what's important is that he went up to her saying: Why don't you answer me, you fucking bitch?! And she went on walking at the same pace, with the same rhythm, with the mist seeming to be clearing a path for her. You father went up to the woman, his hand raised and his penis fully cocked, and then, when she turned her head, she had no human face. Salvador, that woman had thick lips and, behind her veil, the face of a horse.

And then what happened, Mom?

He had sex with her, my boy. And they had a son.

Maternal cackle, then she returned to her flowerpots, crushing orange blossom with her teeth, and rubbing it into Salvador's skin, and the smell made him feel like he was the orange tree.

The dreams of the person who had previously been Salvador became clearer as weariness overcame his body. Childhood opened out like a vivid dream, the thread of the skein unwound and, to his astonishment, completely unedited memories appeared.

María, the daughter of a prostitute, the child whose mother left her tied by the heels when she went to work, was as lovely as the speckled roses in the garden. She grew. And when she was six, and had long hair down below her waist, the eyes of Salvador's father, Vicente, used to follow her everywhere. Don't you like that little girl, Salvador? Wouldn't you like her to be your wife? Just look what a delicious little thing she is. If she's anything like her mother, you won't know what's hit you. No sir. Salvador didn't have the least idea what his father was talking about. Delicious? Delicious like a sweet orange? Or like the corozo fruit when its sweet oil oozed out and his mother would say: Chew the pulp well and don't talk, otherwise you'll choke on it and die. María, with her long hair and that face so full of dignity, was like a strong branch, so straight that, according to his father, you had the impression that one day a very strong wind would come along and, being unable to bend, she'd snap. Vicente whispered in Salvador's ear: Don't you think our little neighbor is lovely? She's like your mother when she was a girl and went around with that ladylike air the whole time. Don't you like her, Salvador? That was followed by a long, loud hoot, the mockery in Vicente's voice, repeating: Salvador likes his little neighbor! Salvador likes his little neighbor! Where was his mother when that happened? In the garden, most likely, plucking a pitaya and pulling off the pieces bitten by bats. Salvador would run outside and stay there beside her for the rest of day. A safe place, far from the paternal screeching. I don't like our little neighbor, he'd say to his mother, and she'd peel him an orange, sit him on her lap for a while, sing him a sad song about an orphaned girl who was engaged to marry a winged creature. I know, son, I know, she'd reply, I know you're not the one who likes our little neighbor, you're four years old, you're not capable of those sorts of desires. And then she'd close her eyes for a time, and when she returned to herself, she'd appear to be putting all her energy into deadheading plants.

His mother said that one day, when she was pregnant with him, she heard a voice coming from her belly. You spoke, Salvador. I didn't know what to do and so I ran outside, but you kept talking to me. Husband, I said to your father when I found him, the child's already speaking and he hasn't even been born. And he, who'd never done anything like that before, was so astonished that he took my word for it and put his ear to my stomach. What can you hear, Vicente? What's he saying? Your father gave me a terrified look. And from then on, he began to gaze into space a lot, he used to stretch out in the shade like an animal and, just like an animal, he enjoyed the feel of the sun and ate grass. Then one day I noticed him looking over the wall at our neighbor. He was watching her the way predators or male animals in the mating season do. What are you up to, Vicente? But your father had stopped speaking by then. He used to spend hours lying in the sun like a dog, like a drunk, and when he wasn't doing that, he was watching the child. She—María— was about four years old then. I always thought you two would get along together, I imagined you both growing up and having children, children that would say: I come from a line of people who have all died feeling grateful for what life has given them. And the children would inherit María's black eyes and obsidian hair. María really loved you, when you were small she'd hold your hands to help you learn to walk. She really wanted you to run. She'd make you grip the orange tree to stand upright and when you got tired, she'd sit with you to make mud pies. Sometimes you ate the pies and the two of you would end up with your mouths full of dirt. We used to take care of María while her mother visited your father. I was never mad, I preferred it to be her coming here than to have him going out God knows where. I also believed that someone had to quench your father's desires before he did something awful, and that's what she did, quench men's desires, and women's too. It was her job, wasn't it? She'd turn up at our house and they'd shut themselves away in our bedroom to do the things I wouldn't. When she came out,

- 204 -

she'd look at me in despair. Has he been biting you again? And María's mother would nod and when I cleaned the wounds, I could see she was crying, her eyes fixed on atrocious visions. In return for that favor, I looked after her daughter. Don't tie her up, neighbor, bring her here and we'll care for her, I said. And you and María became best friends and she'd peel oranges for you, and squeeze the pieces into your mouth so the juice would trickle down without you having to chew. The way grown-up birds do for their little ones, you know. And then, my boy, I died. Do you remember? Your brother Juan arrived and killed me. I didn't want to open the door to him the first time he came. I didn't even want to see him. He knocked and before I had time to ask anything, he introduced himself as one of your father's children. His voice frightened me, I didn't want to open the door. There's nobody called Vicente living here, I said. Years before another boy had come looking for your father, saying he was the son of a dead friend from the time he was a soldier. Right away I knew he was lying, because your father had never really been a soldier, although he could have often passed for one, a soldier without an army. And what's more, that young man was the spit of your father: the same small, sad face, the damp eyes, the high cheekbones, the curly hair. I took him to see your father—he'd just recently gone mad from having heard whatever it was you said to him from my belly and had to be tied up all the time. The young man was so frightened that he didn't ask any questions, and without explaining who he was and why he'd come, he turned to leave. I gave him some fruit for the journey. After that, I knew they would come, one after another, and knowing that soured my milk; you fed from my breasts, and I'm sure you were scared too. That's why I didn't open up to Juan, I didn't want to be frightened. Your father's madness came and went. They said someone had put the evil eye on him, had cast a very strong spell on him, that it was God's punishment for goodness knows what. I don't know, I had my hands full looking after him, there was no time for questions.

One day, when you were small, I went to the bathroom and when I returned, you weren't there. He'd thrown you in the garbage can and your whole body was black and blue. He'd bitten every inch of you, and my anger gave me the strength to tie him up in a darkened room. I wasn't trying to kill him, although by then I hated him. I took him food two or three times a day, tried to talk with him, but your father growled and attacked me. And all that happened because he heard you say something, and even now, when I'm dead, I don't know what it was; those old women in the street who I told what had happened said: Ay, my beauty, you shouldn't have said anything, because if you'd been able to keep the secret, your son would have been a powerful sorcerer, a shaman, or a teller of fortunes. And now you've spoken, my girl, your son will be normal, like the rest of us.

The next time your father turned nonhuman, he bit María. I came home and found her lying in the garden. I'd taken you with me to the market and her mother had left her in your father's care. She must have had some special client, because otherwise I'm sure she'd have chosen to wait for us. The child was purple, her wails had choked her. Her young blood was seeping through her pale dress. I had to slap her to get some reaction. She spent the whole day peeling oranges, not speaking to anyone. After that, her mother took her along with her and you two didn't see each other. I don't know if Vicente was playing the madman or if he really couldn't stop himself turning into a savage dog, eating, running, and lusting like an animal.

Juan had stopped talking to Lázaro's ghost; he talked to the dog instead: Don't you keep hearing laughter, Pigface?

The laughter of things was audible to Juan and they only laughed for him. Everything seemed to be mocking him; in open rebellion, all the elements that made up the world were shaken by terrifying cackles, leaving Juan deafened for a time, staring into the void, which was the only place he could go to stop hearing, stop existing. When he came out of his trance, wanting to take his anger out on something, he'd thrash the dog-body into which Salvador had begun to merge with no hope of return.

When I was a child, Juan said, his fists reddened with his own blood and the dog's (this would also be the only time that the adult Juan would speak of his childhood). When I was a child, I had a dog too, Pigface, only it didn't look like you, it had more fur, a short tail, and honey-colored eyes. It was a present from one of the priests in thanks for my favors; he'd been given the dog by a woman who said it would cure me, because I have to tell you, Pigface, that when I was a boy, I was lame and sickly, and all the doctors, everyone except that woman, said I was going to die. I owe my miserable existence to her. The priest was in despair, possibly because he knew my illness was partly his fault, and when she noticed that, she offered her services; he said he'd found her begging and had brought her back to our church for food and to take a look at me. You should also know, Pigface, that the priest was sometimes generous and tried to reconcile me with life, but by then it was too late for any of us; I realized that the day he gave me the dog after hurting me so badly, leaving me almost dead, and then he said: Keep the dog for yourself, sleep with it, eat with it, talk to it, Juan; it's yours. I knew I'd always be in debt, because when you begin to love something, you owe your life to the world and when you owe something, that something can be a burden. The damned priest even had the nerve to tell me to love the dog well, and the day it died, lame and sick with the same illness I had, it was clear that old man and I were enemies. I begged him to explain, and he told me about the witch and I sobbed, saying he'd taught me that was the same as selling your soul to the Devil. The fool of a priest had exchanged one life for another and that's why I'm still here, Pigface, living my dog's life and very frightened of God; though I'm more afraid of frigging men and so there's no way I'm going to allow them to burn me in the flames here in the desert. I've always been afraid of dying in the desert and being eaten by coyotes. That's not going to happen. When a person is eaten by coyotes, their soul is trapped in the animals' guts. Why do you think they howl that way? And there inside them, you get lost in the labyrinths of their flesh. In there, it's all like the scenes you see in hot coals, it's hell. I've never wanted to go that way. No, sir. I'm going to stay here even if the blood drains out through my feet. Come on, Pigface. Let's keep on moving.

The dog was worn out. And dogs aren't like horses; horses keep on galloping until the moment they become aware of their exhaustion and then they just lie down and die. No, dogs' eyes mist over, they resign themselves in a way that's pitiful to see and the pads of their paws begin to bleed. Salvador had disappeared into the depths of that other body, but childhood had taken root in him like a vivid dream. Here is the boy Salvador, holding on to an orange tree, and María further away in the garden, her eyes wide open, looking at the blue breast of a bird. There's a lack or excess of something human, as though she were an instant away from death and in her face the duration of that moment before death lengthened. With a finger to her lips, she beckons Salvador to look. Don't make a noise, just come here, she says, taking his little arm and helping him to sit beside her. The blue bird hops around on a branch until its breast is turned toward them. Pretty, isn't it? says the six-year-old María, braiding her long hair with long, brown fingers. Do you think God is a man or a woman, Salvo? Do you think death is a man or a woman, Salvo? Do you think there are people who aren't men or women, Salvo? I'm a woman and you're a man, that's right isn't it, Salvo? Will you marry me and have children with me like your mother says? Do you know how babies are made, Salvo? María asks Salvador to go to the darkened room with her. I'll show you something kind of odd, my friend. I've always had it and it looks like a cut, you know? Like when your father bites my mother and makes holes in her skin, says María, glancing down to the floor; that's what it reminds me of. I don't know what it is, but I've got it here and when I touch it, it hurts and I don't like that. And María lifts her dress and there it is, something like a bite mark. I'm really worried, she says, pulling down her dress and taking Salvador's arm to walk to the seat under the orange tree. What time will your mother be back? I wish she was back now, your father's been watching us. María leans over to Salvador's ear and whispers: Aren't you afraid of your dad? I am, Salvo. Your dad is weird.

Oh Lord, whimpered Juan, why couldn't I have had a simple life? He was exhausted from desperately dragging the dog from place to place, and the dog had stopped growling at him now, its eyes were turned up, showing the whites, its head was twisted to one side so thick spittle ran down its chest. Pigface, said Juan, we need to walk on. The dog followed him without complaint. Oh, well, take a rest, said Juan hopelessly, sitting down to once again rub his blistered, stinking feet in the earth. The truth is that he'd been feeling dizzy, and another wave was on its way, he'd felt it coming: the image of the dog was superimposed on that of Lázaro with flies swarming around his eyes as if they were putrid fruit, and then something in Juan shut down. That sensation turned his stomach, hurt him in places he never knew he had: grief was slowly swamping everything he was. Next to that suffering, the pain of the open wounds on his feet was nothing. The blisters and blood from so much walking, the burning skin on his face, his dry, fissured tongue, his hands filthy with ingrained dirt were nothing in comparison to the thing he came up against when he thought of Lázaro and again felt he was standing right on the edge of the concept, the precipice, of death.

He started praying to some invented god, covered his face with his hands and chanted a forgive me Lord, without knowing what lord he was saying it to or why: Forgive me, forgive me.

The dog was still in that deep sleep so like death; it was breathing, although the air scarcely stirred its rib cage. Entombed inside the body of the dog, Salvador continued safe in the protection of his childhood. There, sitting next to him, María made him turn to look at a snake and, hand in hand, the two of them closely inspected the marvelous skin of the lethal animal playing dead before them.

V
Autopsy

Salvador had invited Daniela to watch that movie where an ageing man emerges from the desert. You're going to watch the movie with me, although you probably won't understand it, he said, pulling her down beside him on the couch. But before she'd even had time to get interested in the plot, he was all over her and before the movie could finish she was soaked in their sweat.

Salvador liked putting her open hands over his face; they always had a slight odor of chlorine that made him think of swimming pools.

At times like that, it seemed that he loved her, but then, when it was all over, he'd bite her lip before she could say a word, get out of bed still hot, go to the bathroom and close the door. Daniela would watch him in silence, lying in that position human babies and some animals are born in. All rosy and damp, he'd say when he came out: You look like a newborn piglet.

Salvador liked her because she was servile, she always agreed with him; he liked to be the boss and would say her name when she was about to come as if she were an employee rather than his lover. He talked to her about things he thought she didn't understand, because it made him feel he was talking to himself. In spite of all that, she'd become his best interlocutor and the lover he visited most often. His only lover.

For his colleagues, Salvador was an unknown quantity, they had a sense that his life was solitary and decadent. The smell of damp and old age in the place where he lived, the windows covered in newsprint, his obsession with the nuanced storylines of his movies, were for Daniela a confirmation of that general suspicion. It's not as though she lived in the lap of luxury, but in her cramped apartment there was a clear preference for cleanliness and order.

She had the feeling that something inside Salvador was broken and she thought that the way he used her body might heal that something, that her flesh might distract him from his unhappiness. When she saw him arriving at work, she felt a sort of tenderness not unlike pity snaking about inside her. And she also felt desire, strong desire. She liked the way he spoke for hours at a time about those long stories, and she had a warm feeling when he laughed in his sleep. She wasn't aware that he was pretending to sleep, pretending to laugh, and that when she wasn't there he slept properly and in that deep sleep his teeth chattered and he bit himself.

Everyone in the morgue knew about Salvador's taste for weird movies, he was famous for talking about them while opening up and sewing closed, and for carrying out his tasks with such precision that the almost blind mastery with which he established the cause of death was a little scary. Then, in his spare moments, as if it were quite normal, he'd play with the two gold coins he always had on him, tossing them, catching them, fiddling with them in his pockets.

Daniela found his detachment exciting. Salvador's apparent indifference to the dead bodies made her think he wasn't afraid of anything: he'd talk while he was opening the violated chest of a transvestite with a scalpel, looking up to the ceiling and saying: "A god gave me the power to say how much I suffer."

Do you know what movie that comes from, Daniela? Of course you don't, of course you've never seen that marvelous scene where Elvira recounts her woes in a slaughterhouse: "A god gave me the power to say how much I suffer." A marvelous, a stupendous movie, Daniela.

He loved quoting from movies that no one else had ever seen, that no one else in the morgue would ever see.

Dammit, Salvador, you make it all up, Daniela would say as she used the rubber squeegee to mop away the pinkish liquid pouring from the slab. There were times when she thought him pompous, but she adored listening to him, was moved that he would tell her things about his own life mixed up with the movies and believe she hadn't noticed.

Because Salvador had once told her about himself; he'd said that what he'd really wanted was to study cinema, but he had no money, no family, just a screenplay, a great idea. He wanted to tell the story of a man who lives in the desert until, one day, something alters his peace of mind; movies helped him to forget about reality, and for as long as the show lasted, he left himself behind, was someone else.

He'd started working in the morgue because he needed money to make his first movie, in his own way, using his own resources; a neighbor was a forensic pathologist and one evening, while they were having a drink, he said: Bro, we've been jam-packed lately! You can't have any idea how many people die every day until you see the number of bodies moldering on the slabs, this is serious, we need more workers, but they don't want to fork out for a qualified doctor, so I wondered if you'd be willing to come and help me. You know, setting things up, organizing the bodies, while I teach you how to do what I do; the pay's not too bad, man, and it might just give you inspiration. The craziest thing of all, said Salvador, was that I was good at it, or at least had a special way with death, from habit perhaps, Daniela, it may be just a matter of habit. Then he stood staring at the floor for a while, and, when his spirits rose a little, he looked up again and said: I'm the sort of client who one day realizes they're alone in the theatre at every function.

Daniela waited as if it were her first time, she was surprised to find desire making her inoperative. She made out she was very calm, but Salvador had already sensed how her hands trembled on her squeegee when he adopted that sad intellectual tone to recite:

> . . . he wished he were far away. Lost in a deep, vast country where nobody knew him. Somewhere without language, or streets. He dreamed about this place without knowing its name. And when he woke up, he was on fire. There were blue flames burning the sheets of his bed. He ran through the flames toward the only two people he loved . . . but they were gone.

How about it, Daniela? he finally said one night. Will you have a beer with me and then take in a movie? And, disconcerted by the question, but relieved to have finally heard it, she blushed and quickly removed her latex gloves as a signal that she was coming with him.

He felt that he'd never be able to rid himself of the smell of formaldehyde and so showered before and after going to bed with her. He managed to tolerate his body odor the whole day long with the aid of tobacco. But everything started to look up, a little serenity finally made its appearance after a long night, when Daniela came through the door of the morgue and started to clean with that characteristic air of composure that vanished when she was fucking. During the day, there was a certain rhythm in her hips as she mopped, a movement meant only for Salvador that made him want to pick her up and place her on the slab and do it there and then, surrounded by dead bodies and blood.

During the whole working day, they seduced each other with those small gestures: for his part, while opening up and suturing the corpses, or when he was trying to figure out how the pieces fit together; for her, as she cleaned away the mess, the only job she'd ever had, the only one she knew how to do, because she'd been brought up to serve others. She'd been trained in how to leave dishes and floors sparkling, to leave surfaces so clean they looked polished. One night, her mother congratulated her on that impressive talent and hugged her, murmuring that she was going to be the best cleaner anyone had ever had, thus burning into her soul the idea that she'd been born for nothing other than to leave places spotless. Nobody had ever mentioned any other possibility. It was enough for her to know that no one could beat her when it came to leaving the slab as clean as a new pin. Only Daniela could leave everything perfectly neat and tidy after the arrival of the outcome of that night's slaughter: if it hadn't been for the smell and the evidence, after being cleaned by her, the morgue could have been a kitchen. At least there, the filth was a challenge, although she sometimes felt powerless in the face of the unidentifiable stench hanging heavy in the air that made people walk as though they were levitating, slightly drugged by the formaldehyde or a little downhearted.

And it was there, in that place destined to be dirty, where the game of seduction was played out: bearing gut-wrenching desire for eight long hours, or longer if an unusually large number of bodies were brought in and the shift was extended late into the night. And in those early hours Daniela's magical abilities were needed to maintain the place in a halfway decent state. The two of them would be left alone, neither willing to take the first step, wary of starting to make love there, in the midst of so much killing. Strangely enough, they felt an instinctive need to protect their desires, not to allow them to exist in a place where everything was sullied by misfortune. And that form of superstition would make them hold out all day, all night, until he said: Daniela, are you coming home to see if we can finish that movie? Or: Daniela, if the coin comes up heads, what about it? And with her eyes always lowered, she'd undo her scrubs, and when she looked up, Salvador would think: There's an animal there inside her; because her eyes said it all, anticipating the moment when he'd see her challenging him, enveloping him, naked and almost savage. He'd have the urge to say: Child, my naughty child, and then to slap her so soundly on the rump that the impact would make her breasts wobble.

They both bit their nails and so realized that not even the latex could protect their hands from the scent of death; without saying a word, they would smell, lick, and savor one another, focused on the smell of the deceased, like hungry puppies that don't know hunting is awful, even when it's a matter of survival. Tilting his head back so he couldn't see, she'd put it in. She seemed to want to pull his head off.

Always satisfied, they would sleep as long as they could and then the next day she'd leave before him, because, as he himself put it, she was just a cleaner whereas he was the person who carried out the forensic surgery, and in the morgue was given the respect due to a doctor. Daniela was aware that the impression he created of being a man without fears endowed him with that aura of bureaucratic aristocracy, which meant he was allowed to arrive late. Working with death made him seem to have a higher rank, to be almost a different species.

It was all fine by her. Yes, he was strange; only in bed did he lose that air of debility, that faraway gaze. Anywhere else, his strength consisted of nothing more than that lack of fear. A fragile man, capable of frightening ghosts. Beautiful, even, but with a beauty that came from such profound weariness that it was impossible to be anywhere near him without foreseeing the imminent collapse of his world. On the one occasion when Daniela asked why, she felt she'd come close to precipitating that collapse. His only response was fury.

And so the thread of the secret, the mystery that subjugated the cleaning woman, was cast.

Daniela found herself thinking kitsch phrases like "open up the heart," and laughed at how literal that was; when she was alone, she'd rest her chin on the mop for a moment, reliving scenes from telenovelas where the girl who cleans the house ends up marrying the rich son, scenes that reappeared unconsciously every time she thought she was in love.

If she stopped to think about it, when she was propped up in bed, sitting at the table, or on the couch, she felt something about him was beginning to feel permanent for her. Possibly due to occupational hazards, there were times when he entered her body that she'd close her eyes and wish she could clean from inside herself everything she suspected was putrid in him: she'd concentrate on that idea to the exclusion of all else, as though the violence he exhibited during sex would carry her prayers further. And it seemed to work, because occasionally, when he looked at her, she felt loved. Or it was desire, but a form of desire that seemed longer than any love. Endless. Infinite.

Everything seemed to be going well, but then one night he left the morgue without inviting her to finish watching that movie where the man walks out of the desert toward the highway. The man's demeanor in that scene suggests that he's been lost for years, but has finally found the way out. She'd always get stuck at that point of the movie. The same opening sequences over and over: a desert, a wanderer, and then came the noises, the flesh. She'd return from Salvador's body to another scene with the same man, now telling a girl in black the story of a beautiful woman whom he loved, but then he'd tied a cowbell to her ankle so she wouldn't leave him while he was asleep. Daniela always missed the middle part of the movie. She could never understand how a man who seemed so kindly could have done what he was saying he did: tie up a woman, go drinking, and try to make her jealous. But then it didn't seem so very serious either; in fact, in some way, it was kind of romantic.

She never saw the whole movie, although that day, given Salvador's evasiveness, she tried to get closer to him, using her uncertainties as a pretext. She approached him timidly and almost whispered her question, feeling guilty for asking and not, in her own opinion, being smart enough to understand: Salvador, in that movie we're always watching, why does the man leave if he's found everything he ever wanted?

He walked out without even turning to look at her.

That day they'd brought in the bodies of a boy and a woman. Neither of them had been identified and no one came looking for them. Their bodies were left lying on slabs to be opened by Salvador, who would formally establish the cause of death, even though that was quite clear: they had in common the fact that the person who had murdered them—one in the far north of the city and the other in the far south; that is to say, they were two separate killings—had taken pleasure in tearing apart the center of the bodies. Two men in a single night had attacked two different people with the same level of viciousness. It was known that the culprits were men: the bodies were coated in a filmy white crust. Despite this, Daniela had watched as Salvador opened up the child, whistling a merry tune. He'd also made that signal to which she responded automatically, standing in a way that invited mating. That day, however, she noted that their routine dance seemed to both of them too studied, and each of them switched off, their eyes moving in opposite directions; his fixed on one corner of the room, hers on the spiral formed when she dunked the freshly squeezed mop in the pail. Almost embarrassed, they stopped seeing, and that day desire failed to play havoc on them, leaving them in peace, not looking at each other.

She thought it was because of the boy, that on this occasion, despite being accustomed to such scenes, Salvador had been horrified by the body, although unwilling to admit it.

At the end of the night's work, she watched him, expecting a gesture, a hiss, anything. He headed for the street in his normal clothes, while she, still wearing gloves, was stewing in her yearning to be at least addressed by her name. Without so much as turning his head, Salvador went along the corridor, pulling on his overcoat and lighting a cigarette so languidly that Daniela felt like a ghost. No one looks at me, she thought, no one ever looks at me, and as she said this she realized she was imprisoned; only through that gaze was she was capable of perceiving other eyes. Or it might even be worse: the fact of being looked at by him was all that validated her existence. Except for Daniela, the morgue was by then empty.

She was curious about what Salvador had seen and so approached the bodies.

If that child, thought Daniela as she walked toward the slab, if that child didn't have a bullet wound in his forehead, I'd kiss him right there. She had no idea why she'd thought that. She also tried to figure out what had happened to the boy, but just allowing the question to enter her mind set off an attack of panic that stiffened her arms. She covered the body and then, as if in reflex, moved to the woman, and when she drew back the sheet, despite the cause of her death, found the body so composed, so much a whole, that for some reason she didn't understand she started to feel jealous. She thought of the stories of saints that her mother used to tell her: when their graves were opened, there was a sweet scent. That startled her even more, she experienced a sense of foreboding. How can you feel jealous of someone who's dead? Jealous of a woman who's been raped and murdered and is now lying on a slab in a morgue?

Daniela ran out into the corridor and was seen there by Salvador: she was making the sign of the cross. She fled, haunted by awful visions.

He was hidden outside, fiddling with his two gold coins, tossing them into the air and catching them. He continued like that for a while, and when he was sure nobody was watching, he reentered the morgue.

They didn't even draw a chalk outline around that one's body, the officer who brought in María's corpse had told him.

Her name was María López, and like the daughter of any good prostitute, she only bore her mother's surname; Salvador was well aware of that, but hadn't passed on the information.

You can see she was good-looking, can't you? he said to the officer when they had laid her on the slab and tagged her as Identity Unknown.

He'd made the comment to cover his agitation.

The last time he'd seen her, she was still a child and they used to tell each other secrets. She'd showed him what she called her "cut" and told him: My mother doesn't want to go on seeing your father, Salvo; after what he did, she's frightened of him. We're going away.

She'd uttered those words as if what had happened were the most natural thing in the world.

Salvador hadn't said anything on that occasion either. He'd kissed her cheeks and let her go, without apologies, without pleading: Please forgive us, María, I mean it, please forgive us.

Now, so many years later, it had taken him a few moments to recognize the injured body. Everything about her had grown, although her hair, that hair, was just the same length as in her childhood. Salvador wondered if it was the same hair she'd had as a little girl or if she'd ever had it cut. They say the hair continues to grow after death, he thought, and imagined her in her grave with tresses down to her feet. He saw her there, surrounded by white orange blossoms and attempted to rid his mind of the idea that María, or what was left of her, would be sent to a common grave because she didn't have a name. But he wasn't willing to confess. He wasn't willing to say that the prostitute whose chest it was his task to cut open had been the love of his life and his best friend.

He allowed the men to crack jokes over her body, to talk as if she wasn't there. And he allowed this, knowing (knowing better than anyone) that the newly dead can still hear the comments the living make about them. He said nothing; even went so far as to laugh, to allow the endless necrophiliac humor, the different versions of the same stupid joke the officers told every time they brought in a pretty girl.

Feeling rather disconcerted by his own attitude, he said: Beauty should be recognized, even in death. It was spoken in his characteristic intellectual tone that seemed, just then, imbecilic rather than sad. The retinue of police officers left, still cracking jokes, and only when their voices had faded was Salvador able to feel really alone and, in that solitude, slightly safer. He suddenly sensed the weight of a desiring gaze and knew that Daniela was watching him. He had the urge to say: What are you looking at, you idiot? He hated her, wanted to lunge at her, attack her, but he controlled himself and focused on opening the boy's body. He tried to whistle a song to distract his thoughts (Is it really María?), tried to stick to the routine, to desire. Impossible. Something inside him was going around and around, he felt as if he were falling from a carousel that he'd been securely mounted on his whole life, or as though a parasite had gotten into his brain and was going to make him climb to the top of a high peak and throw himself off.

Once again, María. Once again, her name, like a hammer blow, her voice, the herbal scent of her hair. He couldn't believe she was dead. Ever since those childhood years, he'd been hoping to come across her again, both by then wise, successful, wealthy adults. And until that was true for him, he wouldn't search for her. He laughed to himself: just as she'd promised, she'd found him. Found him there, in that miserable hole where he made himself out to be a man without fears. That was why he decided to pretend to leave. When Daniela had gone, he'd come back to gaze at the woman on the slab, to convince himself that she was his childhood friend, the first woman for whom he believed he'd felt desire, that child who had been forced to become his father's lover. Because deep down, he knew that seeing her would be confirmation of the past, that his memory would drag up what no one had dared to say, but everyone knew. Rather than helping her, he'd assumed that man's ferocious desire, the bite marks he left on María's legs, were normal. He very soon became aware that the blood of that monster ran in his own veins and was now taking over; his penis was pressing against the zipper of his pants, he wanted to enact the desire of a long-dead but still-functioning father. Salvador fiddled with the gold coins and went back inside to say farewell in a way he considered fitting.

The corpses had been taken to a common grave, but when the body of the prostitute passed Daniela, she'd been sure she'd seen a gold coin on each of the eyes.

She also noted that Salvador had stopped looking at her, didn't notice the glances she gave him, the words she spoke to others that were meant solely for him, that alluded to him, that filled her life with their immensity, while he was seemingly completely indifferent to them.

And so the days passed. She devoted herself to cleaning, almost ceremoniously. Her soap turned the blood into sweet, pale pink water.

He'd arrive looking radiant, humming a tune as he opened the bodies, and Daniela finally accepted that it was the radiance of a man in love. He no longer greeted her, didn't tell her the endings of movies. It was as though overnight Daniela had ceased to exist.

Are you seeing another woman, Salvador? It was a straight question. She hadn't been expecting him to smile and reply in the affirmative. How did you know? Daniela was dumbstruck, she went to the room where they kept the cleaning chemicals and furiously banged the door behind her. He knocked. You're not crying, are you, Dani? Irritated, she opened the door. What did the idiot think? Just when did he start referring to her by diminutives? Unable to stop herself, she leaped on him but was incapable of maintaining her fury, just as soon as her skin touched his she wanted to kiss his lips, his whole face.

I love you, she said. Please, take me home with you tonight. He laughed again, doubled up with laughter, and when he stopped to take a breath, said: I thought we were friends, Daniela. You know I have a partner, right? I don't want any problems with her. Then he moved closer and, grabbing her ass, said: Her hair comes down to here. Disconcerted, Daniela responded by hurriedly opening his zipper.

With a grave expression, he calmly removed her hands: Get back to cleaning, I don't have time for this stuff.

Salvador disappeared one day. He simply stopped coming to work. In the morgue it was rumored that he'd run off with his lover, a woman called María, whom he'd suddenly started to mention but whom no one had ever seen. As far as I'm concerned, said one of the police officers, the sly boots made it all up; I don't believe any girl would look twice at such a weird guy; seems to me the fool's gotten out of his depth, all that fucking dead bodies is bad luck, for God's sake, nothing good can come of it. They all laughed. Daniela passed by the officers without giving them so much as a glance.

The person who replaced Salvador was a huge, obese man. He looked more like a butcher than a forensic, always insisting on using the same blood-splattered gown.

She was going downhill fast, because in her eyes Salvador was perfect. The loss of someone that way, a person constructed on idealization and false memories, left her inconsolable. Since the week of his disappearance, Daniela had laid all the blame on herself. It was her fault that he was no longer there, that he'd gone away; she even felt responsible for the vacancy in the morgue and the ineptitude of the fat man who opened up the bodies as if he were a cannibal about to enjoy a banquet.

The last time she and Salvador were together, the sex had been depressing and violent. He'd stopped midway through and run out into the street. While she was dressing to follow him, he returned. She's seen us, Daniela, he said, you have to leave. Who's seen us, Salvador? I didn't notice anybody; come and lie here with me. His eyes were vacant and he hurled insults as he threw her out of the house. She'd been forced to leave, only half-dressed, carrying her boots. Her clothes were soaked in sweat, making her feel the cold. It was a freezing afternoon, the sky was red, up above the sun was like a huge gold Centenario. Daniela thought there might be a quake soon; they said the clouds look like that when a catastrophe is imminent. So many misfortunes that we never know about, she thought as she was leaving, still trying to understand what had happened. She also thought that her god might be following her, announcing her minor tragedy in the sky in that way: something minuscule in relation to the immensity of the universe; her broken heart.

She cried the whole way home and when she lay on her bed, she wrapped herself in the white sheets as if her room were the morgue and she had to play the role of a dead body. She slept deeply, slept for days, only getting up to piss and drink a little water. After a week, she got out of bed and from that time on took to the bottle and returned to cleaning.

She cleaned as if she were cleansing herself. She drank in the same way.

It might look as if she were mopping, but in fact she was washing an infinite corpse.

As the days went by, Salvador took on a more angelic air in her memory, became more handsome and amiable, more complete. Whenever some voice inside her reproached that over-the-top image, she silenced it.

Just when, in her memory, Salvador was no longer Salvador, but another, better man, two bodies were brought into the morgue.

The butcher was disgusted. What sort of animal is this? he asked when the police officers deposited the curled-up body of a man on the slab.

Or at least it had some resemblance to a man.

The officers said the bodies had been brought from some distant village.

You won't believe it, Daniela, said the one who was a master of the suggestive wink, they were brought to us as a special case, they've come from the desert. Who knows how long they were rotting there; two women brought them, saying that one of them had raped her daughters and is now the father of her grandchildren. You had to see that woman, she just went on and on, screaming: Who's going to be responsible for the puppies? I had no idea what she was talking about and simply said, Yes, yes ma'am, we'll send you a report when we've identified the men, and if there's anyone to be responsible for them, you'll be notified at your domicile, so don't come back here, making life hell for us. You know how those ol' ladies are, Daniela, they'll believe anything. When we went to the village to take statements, they said one of the bodies was a dog, the other answered to the name of Juan Barrera and had been living in the desert a helluva long time. They didn't know how those two had met or what the savage was called; because he's a savage man. Haven't you seen him? It's something special, Daniela, I can tell you, never in my whole dog's life have I seen anything like this. But anyhow, there's no case, because the ones who seem to know most about it all are the boys. It was one of them found the bodies of these two wretches. When we took his statement, one boy said: Señor Juan's dog did something bad to my sister, so me and my friends decided to go looking for them, we even brought torches, we wanted to hunt the beast and set up a circus to show him. Those damn kids are wrong in the head. I dunno. Anyway, you just tell the doctor here to examine them, then they're off to the common grave, and that's the end of the whole business. I don't care if it was the Devil or the savage, I couldn't give a fuck about those damn yokels, Daniela, they're ignorant peasants . . .

As Daniela was drunk, she soon stopped listening to the officer and sunk into the hazy memory that was in fact her own invention of Salvador's naked back, more muscular, more elegant; so much more than it had ever really been. She came back to the real world when the officer, in some strange act of coquetry, took her hand and led her to the slab. I want you to look, Daniela, he said. I want you to look at this bastard and tell me what the hell it is: man or dog. I haven't the first idea.

Apparently, after the savage's death someone had taken the time to close its eyes. The eyes of the other man were, however, wide open, as though he could still see. There was no way the fatso could lower his lids. He finally put a piece of cloth over them so he didn't feel he was being watched, and then started to work on the body. After a while, he informed Daniela: According to the test results, these two were half brothers.

When Daniela first saw Salvador lying on the slab, she didn't recognize him. Something about him was familiar, but she was still convinced that Salvador, her Salvador, was alive somewhere, lying naked next to María. And that, despite so much fucking and so little sleep, they were both perfect.

The press was obsessed by the case, many people were discovered trying to peer through the bars of the windows. For weeks, headlines in the city's newspapers included the word "savage." The interest was at fever pitch when the bodies of Juan and Salvador were, despite their fame, to be taken to the common grave. They are unnamed; that's all we can do for them, said the boss.

In the office, Daniela read the incredibly well-spelled report telling the story of the old woman who had brought the body to the morgue:

We put the bodies of Señor Juan and his dog in the back of my son's pickup and took them to the police, hoping to find someone to help us. The dog got my daughters pregnant and we can't afford to bring up so many creatures. We didn't want those men dead, they ran off and we just followed the boys when they said they'd found the bodies. The whole village had been looking for them to talk to Señor Juan about his beast's misbehavior, but the boys always know the desert better when they're on horseback. So it was them who found Juan and the dog lying there in the middle of nowhere, their feet all cut, their faces fried to a crisp by the sun. We'd thought that the dog could pay the upkeep of the creatures by joining the circus we'd set up on a cart, but we hadn't counted on finding it dead. We didn't kill the dog, we think Señor Juan throttled it, because it has the mark of a leash around its neck. We think Señor Juan died later of thirst because his tongue is white. We also think that they both have a pact with the Devil. God save us and save my new grandchildren from their father's curse. The children have come out well, thanks be to God, and even look like humans. So don't go accusing us of any crime, the village is only guilty of having allowed such monsters to live among us. We politely ask you to leave us in peace, not to come to our village looking for the murderer, because those men killed each other and we're not to blame for that. We'll have our work cut out trying to cleanse our children of the fright; the lucky ones held their breath when they found the corpses, otherwise, officer, the souls of those wretches would have already invaded them.

The obese pathologist hadn't been able to break the rigor in the bodies. They'll have to go naked, he said. Daniela knew about the trick Salvador had used to relax his patients, but she didn't have the courage to say to that lardcake: My friend, you have to whisper in their ears and ask them to rest. She just didn't dare.

The controversy had died down by then and, in the true scientific spirit, the doctors maintained that the savage man was in fact one of those filthy locos thrown out from psychiatric clinics into the street. In terms of the relationship between the two men, they came to no conclusion. It was noted that the difference in their ages was unusual in brothers. And that was all. In the morgue, the case garnered less interest, because bodies went on piling up on the slabs and there were always fresh priorities. They kept the corpses until the limit for someone to come and claim them had passed. It was the best they could do; those slabs were needed.

Daniela approached the savage one last time. His body was so tightly curled that the face was almost hidden. They had said it was impossible to change the position, but she'd waited for a moment when no one else was in the morgue to see if she could repeat what Salvador managed to do when he leaned over to whisper to the corpses, saying things that apparently calmed them and loosened up their muscles.

I don't know your name or where you come from, but your time has come. Surrender, said Daniela. She looked all around to ensure that no one could see her casting her spell. The body, however, didn't relax. She had to move closer and repeat: Your time has come; surrender.

Her tone was more threatening than calming, but, despite this, it seemed that something in him was changing. She knew she had to move even closer, that her lips had to brush the corpse's ear. Her stomach churned, but some powerful force she couldn't put a name to urged her on.

And then, she saw him. She saw Salvador in the body of the savage. She immediately felt as though the alcohol were burning her guts and ran to the bathroom to throw up a stream of bitter, yellow vomit.

It can't be true, she said. And she mentally conjured up an image of Salvador that had no resemblance to the hunched savage on the slab. In her perfect, almost brilliant mental image, he was putting an arm around her waist, saying over and over: Surrender, you bad girl. But her memory substituted the image of herself with a brown-skinned woman, the spit of the dead prostitute she'd once felt jealous of, and she, they, the two women, as one, rocked back and forth over Salvador, both of them naked and full of life, while everything smelled not of blood, not formaldehyde, but of roses.

It was still quite early when Daniela washed her face, rinsed away the vomit, picked up her purse, and left the morgue.

In a village in the desert, a story is told of two men; it's said that in one of the houses the children of a savage man are fed on goat's milk. No one ever speaks, and never will speak, of how the entire village came together to steal and strip a certain car to sell for spare parts; they might just mention the adventures, the juicy details of what they imagined to be the lives of a man and a strange dog, say they dragged themselves along like lunatics to die under the desert sun. The story will at times become the legend of a travelling circus, at others of a pair of apparitions; the ghosts of Juan and the dog will be the usual suspects in any murder and, with no one knowing quite why or how, children and old people dreaming the dreams of second childhood will introduce into their tales the character of a trader who awaits the unwary at the side of the road to offer them gold and truths. And when they have to pass Señor Juan's abandoned house, mothers make their children hold their breath, make them take off their clothes and put them on again inside out, in order to prevent the spirit of Juan or the dog entering them and eating their souls.

For years, but not forever, Salvador will appear in Daniela's dreams as a sad, lustful hero: she will give up her body to him, despite the slight smell of death on his skin.

ACKNOWLEDGMENTS

I would like to thank the Fundación Antonio Gala for their support in the early stages of writing this novel.

My thanks also go to:

Pablo Villalobos, Guillermo, and Vania for their generous collaboration.

My friend Otakame, who is always there when needed.

To the Gutiérrez siblings and to Alejandro, the conversation during the journey toward the ending of this novel, the sea, the desert, the winged horse, the coral snake.